FROM
Darkness
TO
God's Light

BONNIE WERNER

Just finished your story, what a life!! I felt like I was walking along with her the whole time. Great testimony to the mercy and power of our gracious God!

—Diana Baker,
Middletown, MD

Honestly Bonnie I must commend your novel because you really did well writing this novel. This is a wonderful novel that will impact knowledge to the entire world. Thank you so much for sharing this great story and may God bless you so much. I pray that God in his infinite mercy fortify you to continue with this wonderful work to help humanity.

—Darren Ancelotti,
Dusseldorf, Germany

I found this book to be very interesting. When I first started to read it, it seemed to go slowly, but as I kept reading, it intrigued me more, and I couldn't put it down.

It was so neat to watch how God worked in Babs' life, and turned her around from her sinful nature, and started using her as a Witness to others.

I could especially relate to the places mentioned in the book. It made me feel like I was right in the middle of the story!

Bonnie did a good job on giving Babs' testimony for the Lord. We can all relate to that part in our lives when we were in the dark, and finally saw the light.

This book will be such a good witness for others. I hope Bonnie keeps up the good work!

—Ellen Harris,
Raymore, MO

CONTENTS

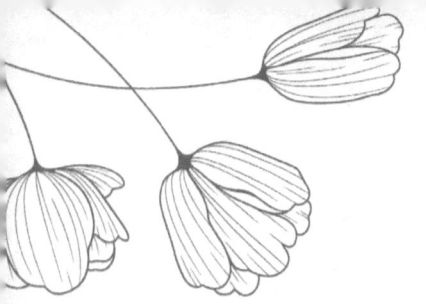

PART I

CHAPTER 1

Pushing the Boundaries

"Hello, Greyhound? You have my suitcase!"

"When I got off the bus, I handed my ticket to the driver, but he just closed the door and left! With my bag still on the bus!"

"No, I don't have the number, I gave the ticket to the driver!

"You have to talk to the driver, it's the bus from St Louis to Fort Meade. I just got off the bus, and no one's here, everything's closed. Can you please help me get my suitcase?"

Babs dialed the payphone again.

"Hello, George G. Meade Education Center? May I speak to Ronald Weston, he's just finished A School and I'm here for his graduation tomorrow. I really need to speak to him, please?"

Pause.

"Ronnie, Oh I'm so glad I could get you on the phone, I'm actually here! I'm all alone at the bus stop and everything's closed, so it's dark, and I need you!"

"Yes, I got the bus this morning like we talked about, and I miss you! But the bus drove off with my bag! I'll have to call them with a number where they can reach me tomorrow. Will they let you come get me to bring me to the base? Well, can you borrow a car? Okay, good. I'll just sit here on this bench and wait for you. Thank you, honey!"

Babs had left the house Friday morning telling Mother that she was spending her weekend off work with a friend from work, who said she'd cover for her. Ronnie had joined the Navy while she was still in high school, and when he finished Boot Camp they sent him directly to Maryland to learn how to be a radio operator. Now he finished that with flying colors, and she was so proud of him!

But her real reason was that she wanted to get out of that authoritarian house! Now that she graduated and found a job downtown, she was tired of hearing, "You can't do it because I said so, and I am the parent here!" When Ronnie had told her he could have guests for his graduation, she immediately bought a bus ticket and took off. It was so exciting!

When she got back home Sunday night, Mother was livid! She had called the friend's house, and Sally's mother had answered the phone, and blew her cover!

"Barbara Jane Mellen! Where have you been? Your father and I have been worried sick over you!"

"But, Mother, Ronnie finished his A School training and they said he could have guests, so I had to be there for his graduation!"

"Why didn't you tell us where you were going? Why did you make up that story?"

"Of course, I couldn't tell you where I was really going, I knew you wouldn't let me go because we're not married yet! But it was all right, they put me in the guest quarters, anyway!"

"But anything could have happened to you, going off alone like that!"

"Oh, I was perfectly safe on the bus for that 12 hours; I wasn't alone, I talked to a guy I sat next to the whole way."

"And Ronnie and I came back together after. Nothing was going to happen to me!"

Honestly, her parents thought that they had to keep her under their thumb! She still couldn't do anything or go anywhere without their permission. Mother said that she didn't want her to make mistakes with her life, so she was to only do what Mother and Daddy approved of. But really, they just wanted to exert all the authority! And they didn't even agree, it was easy to play one off the other.

Babs had told Mother that she wanted to make her own mistakes, and that upset her. But she had graduated from high school and had a job downtown, and she wanted to be free from all the constraints. Babs was grown up now and didn't want to listen to anyone! This was the sixties, and attitudes were much more relaxed than they had been in the fifties. She was smart, and could make her own decisions for herself, and she couldn't wait to get out of that house!

She still couldn't even wear the clothes she liked. When she had put on her short-shorts and crop-top when she started to develop, Daddy told her to, "Put on something more modest!" Mother told her he said that because they "caused a problem" for him. This was at least one area they could agree on. But these clothes attracted the attention of guys, and they told her she was pretty. She had asked Daddy back then if she was pretty, and he just said, "Of course you are, all my girls are pretty!" But she didn't think all her sisters were pretty. At that time Marilyn Jo was a buxom blonde teenager with flashing green eyes, and Babs thought she was beautiful; but her other big sister Dana had dark brown hair and eyes, and was still at the in-between stages and Babs didn't consider her very pretty yet. She herself had dish-water blonde hair and blue eyes, and her little sister Janet had light brown hair and brown eyes, but she was still a kid, so she didn't count. So, she couldn't trust Daddy's answer.

Now Ronnie told her she was beautiful. And he liked her skimpy clothes, they turned him on, and he got so romantic.

But when he left to go to overseas, she was alone again. They wrote letters, but it wasn't the same. At the phone company they put her on a split-shift, working four hours on, four hours off, and back on the other four hours. Since she lived a half-hour bus ride from downtown, Babs decided to stay in town in between, so she went with the girls to volunteer at the USO, the United Service Organization that helps the troops when they're away from home, where they could meet guys. That was fun.

Now that she was getting a taste of life, she left that childish attitude of trying to "obey all the rules." She could bend them a little, and have some fun, and still be "good enough" to not worry about going to hell. She wouldn't be that bad!

When Babs had been in the Catholic high school, she tried to do everything right, and obey all the rules. She knew she wasn't perfect, but she refused to do anything really bad. And she even tried to avoid the little "sins," following the guidelines her church taught. And all the other students and teachers around her kept her straight. So, she was set!

But now that she was free from those constraints, she was having fun. What good was life without a little fun? And boyfriends were a lot of fun!

When Ronnie came home again, he just didn't understand, and he had been with other girls while he was away, so they broke off the engagement and agreed to be just friends and date others.

That's when she met Tom. He was so handsome in his Army uniform. So, they started to date.

"Hey, Babs, there's a carnival in town, want to go?"

"Yeah, sure, that sounds like fun."

They arrived at the fairgrounds while it was still light, and they started walking down the grand boulevard with all the games.

"Win me that big bear, would you, sweetie?" Ker-plunk! "Oh, that's okay, you don't have to be good at everything!"

Soon the sun set, and the whole park lit up.

"Oh, Babs, look at that huge Ferris Wheel!"

"Tom, I hate Ferris Wheels, you know I'm scared of heights!"

"I'll be right beside you, honey, it'll be alright!"

"Well, keep your arm around me and don't let it rock!"

They stepped into the gondola and began the ascent, to spin around, up and down, which wasn't too bad; then it slowed down to start to let people off.

And of course, they stopped at the very top!

"Hey, Babs, look behind us, you can see all the lights of the whole carnival, it's beautiful!"

"Tom, Tom, you're rocking it, I'm afraid I'll fall! Please be still!"

Babs was white-knuckled on the hand-bar until they were back down on solid ground! Then she vomited on the leg of the Ferris Wheel! This was serious!

"Oh, I'm sorry, Babs, I didn't realize how afraid you were. It won't happen again."

Yeah, right! Later when they crossed the walk-bridge over the highway, he made like he'd throw her over! "Eeeah!" She squealed as she dropped to the pavement! "But I was only kidding!"

Tom thought she was so cute in the clothes he bought her, but she had to put them on after they left the house. He didn't like the constraints any more than she did, so he arranged for Babs to rent an apartment downtown, not far from work. He was staying on base, just across the river in Illinois. Whenever he could, though, he stayed with her in the apartment.

"Hey, Babs, I'm getting a week off—let's go up to Green Bay and I'll introduce you to my parents. You've got a vacation coming, don't you?"

"You want me to meet your parents?"

"Well, yeah. I love you, Babs, let's get married while we're up there. Will you marry me?"

"Married? Oh, Tom, you're so sweet!"

Since they only had a week they found a justice of the peace in the Upper Peninsula of Michigan to the North, where they didn't have to wait another week, like in Wisconsin, and his parents were the witnesses. She didn't get the big wedding she always wanted, but she had a husband now, so it was okay. Now that she was married, life would go wonderfully!

When they got back to his parents' house, her new mother-in-law said, "Well, I suppose you'll want clean sheets on the bed!" as she handed Babs the linens, to make her own wedding night bed, in Tom's childhood bedroom! The next day, Mom sat Babs down, knowing that she was Catholic, and tried to witness to her saying, "Mary and Joseph had other children after Jesus was born, you know!" This family she just married into was Baptist! They believed the whole Bible, but the Catholic church ignores a lot of it, to teach their own Traditions.

Her new mother-in-law knew that the Catholic church didn't teach that part of the Bible, and was probably wanting to start a conversation about it.

But Babs had never heard this before, and thought she was just attacking Babs' faith. Now she felt like she had to defend it! "No, Mary is Ever-Virgin, and she and Joseph had a chaste marriage!" She repeated what she'd been taught.

Babs had no idea why she had to bring that up! Was she trying to cause a fight, right away? It didn't make sense to her at the time, she wanted to get along with her new family. But God used it later in Babs' thinking.

CHAPTER 2

The Slippery Slope into Darkness

When they got back to St. Louis, Tom sat Babs down. "Now that we're married, I'll tell you that I was married before, and we had two kids. But my wife wasn't faithful to me, and I divorced her. I lost the kids because my wife was deemed an unfit mother, and I needed my mother to care for them while I worked nights, and she didn't think the little boy was mine, after catching her with my best friend. Here's a picture of them. They were adopted out."

"Why didn't you tell me about this before, Tom?"

"Well, Babs, I wanted to be sure you wouldn't consider me out of your league and break up before we could be married!"

"You don't know how much I love you? You didn't trust me to stay with you if I knew the truth about you?"

"Well, I couldn't trust my first wife."

So, Babs found out that she wasn't his first wife, and that he was over seven years older than her (he'd lied about that), and that he didn't think he could trust her! Three red flags, and now she was stuck!

A few weeks later they had their first fight.

"Babs, honey, where were you last weekend while I was stuck on base? I tried to call you, but you never answered the phone all weekend! Do you have a boyfriend or something?"

"A boyfriend? What are you accusing me of, Tom? You were going to be gone all weekend, so I went to visit my folks. I was at their house. Why would you accuse me like that!"

"Well, I expect my wife to be at home where I can reach her!"

"Tom, you're acting like I'm your property that you own, instead of your equal other half! You weren't even going to be here, and I didn't want to sit around all alone, so I went to visit with my family. You could've called me there."

"But I didn't know where you were. I was just worried about you, honey, and I'm angry that you would go see your parents who didn't approve when we told them we were married, so I'll sleep on the couch tonight!"

"Oh Tom, don't do that! I missed you all weekend, and I want you to come to bed! Come on, I'll make it so good for you!"

"No, this will teach you a lesson!"

Oh, this was just great! Babs thought that having a husband would solve all her problems, but marriage was becoming even more problematic and painful than living with her parents!

Then a couple of months later, Tom came home with orders for Viet Nam! No one from this base had been sent over there, but the war was escalating so, he had to go.

"I only have two weeks, so I'm going to move you up to Wisconsin so my parents can keep an eye on you while I'm gone. They live in the country, so I'll find you a place to stay in town, and you can transfer your job at Southwestern Bell to the Green Bay office. My sister lives in town there, you can make friends with her."

Oh, wow, now he's going to plan out her life for her! Well, Tom will be on the other side of the world for who knows how long, and Babs will be on her own, fancy free! Now she'll be able to live her own life however she wants.

She was able to rent a room in a beautiful old house, upstairs with the shared bathroom down the hall. And she had Tom's car that his folks kept for him, so now she needed to learn how to drive. She enrolled into a drivers' ed course, and they picked her up and dropped her off. After six lessons, she was eligible to take the driver's license test, and she passed. Now with license in hand, she could "practice" driving all she wanted, to get the experience the instructor told her she needed.

Now she was free! Babs made friends with all kinds of people, and she was able to go wherever she wanted and do whatever popped into her head! And since Tom was on the other side of the world, when she got lonely she could find comfort in other arms.

The wife of one of her guy friends was a fun gal, so when Babs bought a ring for Tom for his birthday, she stopped by Shirley's work to show her the gift before she mailed it off, and Shirley said, "Hey, Babs, you ought to go talk to my boss, Sam, about getting a job with us. We're a talent agency and we book dancers in clubs. You'd make a terrific go-go girl! And you'd make a lot more money than you're getting at the phone company."

"But, Shirley, I don't know how to dance. I can only do the jitter-bug that my big sister taught me so she could practice it after seeing it on American Bandstand."

"We can show you; I can tell you'd be good at it by the way you move when you walk. Here, can you do this? And this?" as she moved her hips in a sexy, back-and-forth movement, with a pouty-face.

"Sure, easy-peasy."

This really looked like a lot of fun. She could go out every night drinking and dancing and get paid for it! Life was starting to look good!

She could still work as a telephone operator days and go out dancing at night, and if she worked it right, she could save some money. When her two work schedules conflicted, she went full-time dancing, all over the northern Midwest in seven different states, and realized she could sleep with a different guy every night if she wanted.

She wrote to Tom that she was dancing, and since he didn't think he could talk her out of it, he suggested a "stage name" for her that she thought sounded like a horse!

And that old car threw a rod, so she was back on the bus again.

But now she'd be able to save enough money to take that honeymoon they couldn't afford before, by the time Tom finished his tour and got out of the Army. She still wanted to be that good little girl that had married him.

She would quit dancing and find an apartment in a different neighborhood, where he wouldn't be likely to meet any of her boyfriends, and clean up her lifestyle. Maybe they could even start a family. She could maybe even start back going to church, too.

But when Tom came home, he spent her honeymoon money on another car instead, because he had to have something to drive, so there was no honeymoon. Another disappointment. And he got the job back at the factory where his dad worked.

"Hey, Babs, since you're not working and I'm back at the factory, I'm not making enough money to buy you all the nice things I want you to have. Why don't you call Sam and see if you can go back to dancing? You make more money doing that than I do on the line."

Then he thought again, and said, "And maybe I can quit this job, too, and go with you, if Sam will hire me as an agent, recruiting other girls to dance like you? Then we can still be together."

If they could be together, that would keep her from sleeping around anymore. That might work. But she had a question for him: "Tom, you say that you're a Christian, but you want to talk girls into what can be an immoral lifestyle?"

"Yes, of course I'm a Christian! I walked the aisle to the altar to accept Christ when I was twelve years old and I cried!"

"And what do you mean by, "immoral"? They don't have to drink too much or do anything else but just dance sexy on a stage!"

The Agency hired him as an agent, but right away, Sam sent Tom to Florida for a week to check out if the situation down there was worth moving the agency out of the winter weather, while Babs was dancing in Minnesota. So, they weren't even together like she expected.

CHAPTER 3

Into the Void

Sometimes Tom was with Babs while she danced, but when he wasn't, she still had her one-night-stands and boyfriends. She couldn't seem to not be attracted by all the attentive guys, and what Tom didn't know won't hurt her!

One guy who liked her dancing took her out for breakfast after the bar closed and they spent an enjoyable night together, then in the morning, he took her driving in his luxurious sport car. "Wow, this is really nice! What is it, a Porsche? I love red convertibles."

"You like this car? Would you like to have this car? I will give it to you, and you can drive it home instead of taking the bus. It can be yours, free and clear."

"Give it to me? You mean you'll just sign it over to me, for free?"

"Sure, you like it, don't you; it can be yours!"

"No, I can't take it; what would I tell my husband? It would be too suspicious." And she didn't want Tom to suspect anything, he was so possessive. "But let's see how fast it will go!" And they took it out for a spin.

"Oh, these mountain views are beautiful! And it's so exciting driving with you, Lloyd; you're so much fun."

"And you're fun to drive with, sweetie! Oh, oh, oh, we almost slid there! Wow, we almost went right off this high mountain road; we were going too fast around that curve!" Then he said something unexpected, "Somebody must have been watching out for us, I don't know how we stayed on that overhanging cliff! Babs, honey, you weren't even scared! You are one cool cucumber!"

Angels must have been surrounding the car, keeping it from driving off the mountain into certain doom.

Babs was so oblivious she hadn't even realized the danger until it was over.

But it got her thinking. She really must clean up her act and fly right, or Tom would find out about all these guys.

Then one week while she was dancing in Wausau and he was able to be with her, she offered, "Oh, Tom, it's so nice when you can travel with me as I dance. Look, it's Sunday, do you want to go to church? We can find one of your churches here?"

"No, I just want to sleep in this morning, you go ahead if you want."

So Babs found a Catholic church not far from their hotel and decided to go. Maybe she could meet someone there she could talk to and help her change her ways. She was coming to think that maybe that she wouldn't be able to do it on her own, without outside pressure.

She decided to sit in the back, then she could come out first and make friends with whoever wanted to meet her. "Hi, I'm new here ..." "Hello, I'm ..." "Good morning ..." "Wasn't that a good sermon..." Why is nobody even looking at her? They are all just walking past her as though they don't see her and gathering into their little threes and fours together on the patio. Well, the priest will be glad she came. "Good morning, Father!" But he didn't notice her, either; he just looked toward his people and conversed with each little group. Maybe God had made her invisible to these people because He didn't want her in this church.

She thought, "Isn't God supposed to be Love? Aren't we supposed to love each other? There's no love here. They're all just concerned with their own little cliques. The God of Love is not in this Catholic church!"

Babs figured that if God wasn't in that church denomination anymore, then has what she's been taught all her life even true? What is Truth?

CHAPTER 4

Spiraling Downward

Babs bought a Bible: it was supposed to be God's word. Maybe she could find the answer there. When she read a book, she always started at the beginning and read every word to the end. So, she started to read it. All these Bible stories sounded familiar, and they were interesting to read.

She even read a chapter out loud to the guy who came up to her room after dancing that night! The next night at the bar, his wife came storming in, accusing her of adultery with her husband because he called out "Babs!" in his sleep! Babs told her that his dreams were his own imagination, and that they didn't do anything last night but read the Bible together! That was a real hoot! Good thing she hadn't actually slept with that one!

She got pretty far into this Book, but when she got past the stories and got into a whole passel of begats, she didn't understand what it all was supposed to be about. All these people having sons that have sons that have sons were only names, names she couldn't even pronounce, and nothing about any of these people.

There was chapter after chapter of these lists! She couldn't skip this much of a book, so she put it down, and decided to investigate other kinds of belief systems.

One night one of the other dancers held a séance in their hotel room to try to contact the spirits around them, and she told Babs that she could see her aura and that it showed that something wasn't right in her midsection, and that she should seek medical attention.

"You're right—I have a urinary tract infection, and I am on medication for it." That was amazing!

There might be something to this. Maybe there are spirit beings around us who can communicate with us. There must be some kind of help out there. She couldn't talk to Tom, he'd just get mad, and she was still travelling from city to city each week dancing. Maybe there are good spirits out there who could help her, if she could only find them.

She started to read books about spiritual beings, hauntings and poltergeists and ESP and Astrology, and anything paranormal, and they all looked so interesting. These ideas pulled her into also getting a deck of Tarot cards and a Ouija board.

But none of these things was doing anything to help her to not be unfaithful to Tom. Nothing she found seemed to be able to break her addiction to one-night-stands. Every time she tried to do better, she just ended up falling into bed with the next guy.

She really wanted to make this marriage thing work, but she seemed to be destroying it herself! What could she do?

Then came the week she was performing with another dancer at a hotel in Madison. Tom came in for their last night and got his own room down the hall from the dancers' room paid for by the hotel. This was nice, they could spend the day together. It was a beautiful spring day, and as they walked through the park-like setting, Tom told her it reminded him of when The Rapture would occur.

"'Rapture'? What's that?" That's a word she never heard in a Catechism class, or anywhere else in the Catholic church. It must be Baptist.

"It's when Jesus comes to call out His people, and we will fly up into the sky to be with Him."

"Is that in the Bible? Can you show it to me?" She knew that he went by the Bible.

"Yes, it's in the Bible, but I don't have one with me right now, just trust me." Well, if he couldn't show her, maybe he could tell her about it.

"Fly up into the sky? You mean like with wings or an airplane or something?"

"No, just in our bodies."

"Ha, ha, you mean fly up into the air just like that? What an amusing picture I'm seeing, with people just flying up into the air all over the place!"

"You're laughing at me! You're laughing at my Bible!" and he stormed off!

"Wait, I'm only laughing at the picture in my mind!" *sigh* "Oh well, it's useless. I can't even talk to him! I don't think this marriage is worth working on anymore. I'm going to leave him tonight."

That night was the last night of her gig at that hotel, and the dancers didn't have to be out of their paid room until morning. Tom decided to watch the Packers game on TV while Babs danced downstairs, so every break she had to change costume, she'd pack a little in her suitcase, then bring another drink to him in his room. By the end of the evening, she had everything packed, and her roommate, the other dancer, had booked a third room for her to spend that night in on another floor.

When Tom expected her to stay with him in his room, she knew he'd tie her to the bedpost if he knew she was leaving him. So, she told him, "I just need to get my toothbrush, you know I have to brush my teeth before I leave the room in the morning. I'll be right back." But she wasn't.

She padded up the hall, and said, "Ok, I've got my suitcase and the key to my other room. Thanks for helping me with this. When Tom comes looking for me, just act surprised, and say you thought we were leaving tonight, and you don't know where I am."

When she got upstairs to her extra room, she immediately called Sam to tell him what was going on, and not to tell Tom anything! To just say that he'd booked her somewhere he hadn't, because Tom would rush there and make a scene!

When the other dancer gave Tom the story, he realized that she wasn't coming back to his room that night. Tom was so upset, he immediately got fully dressed in his three-piece suit and tie and sat in the lobby all night, because: "I know she'll have to come through here to get out of the hotel."

When he finally left the hotel in the morning to drive back home, Babs called him before she checked out to tell him she'd left him.

"No, I didn't leave you for any other guy, I just left. I don't love you, Tom, and I don't think this marriage is working."

"Where are you now?"

"I'm in Milwaukee at a friend's place." A lie. That was a big city where she'd never been.

"Some guy?"

"No, a girl friend."

"We don't know anybody in Milwaukee."

"I know a lot of people you don't know. Don't try to look for me, you won't find me. Goodbye, Tom."

Now she really was free. But was she?

Even having left Tom, she was becoming more determined to try to do better on the moral front, to not just fall into bed with every desirable guy she met, but she just didn't know how.

At the next gig she met Larry. He was the scion of a huge construction empire and was in line to inherit it all when he finished at Harvard. He was probably Satan's distraction from her search for the Truth.

"Hey, Babs, you're a lot of fun. Why don't you marry me, and we can have a blast together!"

"Well, I could divorce my husband, since he's not divorcing me." Larry might be able to keep a reign on her, and he was wealthy.

"Great, my family lawyers can take care of that; but to be accepted by my family, you have to have a degree, did you go to college?

"No, but I could."

"I can get a degree for you from whatever college you want; how about Radcliffe?"

"Just the degree on paper? I'd rather go ahead and take the courses to earn it!"

"Okay, we'll marry when you graduate; and you can have all the boyfriends you want on the side, as long as you're discrete, like me."

"But, Larry, if we get married, wouldn't you want me to be true to you, and faithful?"

"Come on, Babs, you're not serious! How can you say that? Get real!"

Babs didn't want to disrespect Marriage as she had been doing, so leaving Tom eased her conscience a little on that level, so she was able to have a really good time with Larry that week. But if he wouldn't even consider the seriousness of the bond of Marriage that she was realizing, then marrying him wouldn't give her any help at all to force her into doing right, even with his fortune.

When Larry showed up at her next gig, in the next town, he ignored her, because she hadn't jumped on his train. He wouldn't even buy her a drink!

Where was this going? Every time she wanted to do better, she just ended up falling into bed with the next guy. How could she break out of this downward spiral?

When Sam sent her up to Montana, she met a cowboy who worked the oil rigs. Raul Hocker wasn't very tall, just an inch or so taller than Babs' 5'4" but he was really built, and he convinced her to come with him to West Texas where he could get work. She'd never been to Texas, and it was way out of her agency's territory for dancing, but he wasn't worried about being able to support her, so she quit and took off with him.

When they got to Odessa, he went early to the spot where the oil guys chose their teams for the day, but it seemed that he didn't get there early enough most days. So, he sent Babs to the Albertsons Grocery and showed her how to hide stuff under her coat. She was concerned because she'd read about some poor father of six who was sent to jail for stealing peanut butter! If she was going to get caught, it would have to be for the best steaks in the deli.

The weather was starting to get a little chilly, so she put on her big, bulky coat and headed off to the store. She started off "shopping" in some of the aisles, then moseyed off toward the meat counter. Perusing all the prime cuts, she chose several of the biggest and best steaks they had, and surreptitiously sequestered them under her armpits. Then she wandered about again among the aisles and left the store. No one followed her out! She got away with it!

Babs and Raul ate good that night. But it didn't last long. Raul said that he couldn't get any work there because the other guys all beat him to it. So, they needed to go somewhere else.

This was getting old. They were out of money and out of food and he asked her if she knew anyone who would lend them some cash. Babs knew her father wouldn't approve of her lifestyle, even though her folks had split up and he'd remarried. But she called Daddy anyway, telling him she just wanted to go home. He probably saw through her lie, and responded with, "After you clean up your act, then call me and I will be willing to help you. But not until then." Well, if she could clean up her act, she wouldn't need his help!

So, that left Tom.

"Oh, Tom, honey, I'm so sorry I left you! I want to come home to you. Please send me some cash so I can buy a ticket back and some food to eat on the way!"

"Good work, Babs, there's a wire coming in for you!" He must have swallowed her story.

"Oh, but Raul, it's not cash, it's a ticket from here to Wisconsin! There's no other funds attached."

So she dialed him again. "Tom, honey, thank you for the ticket. But it's a three-day trip, what am I supposed to eat on the way? Can you send me some cash, too?"

"No, Babs, my brother-in-law would only send the ticket. If you want to come home, come home. You'll be okay." So he had to ask his sister's husband.

"But I'll starve on the way!"

"Sorry. Take it or leave it." And he still didn't trust her, with good reason, now

"Raul, what're we going to do? We have no money, and only one bus ticket from here to Wisconsin that we can't cash in."

"Well, Babs, we can sleep in the bus station tonight, and I'll put you on the bus in the morning. And I'll see what I can do to meet up with you later. Here, you can take this packet of peanut butter crackers we have left to eat on the bus, I'll find something."

"Thank you, Raul. I'll get off the bus at the St. Louis terminal, and go to my mother's house."

So, that's what she did. And she ended up right back where she started.

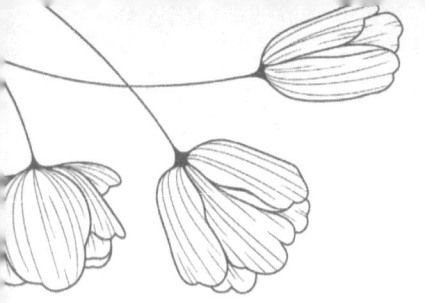

PART II

CHAPTER 5

The Way Out of the Tunnel

Back home was so much different than when she left it. It had been an intact, nuclear, two-parent family, even if it was a bit dysfunctional with arguing parents. When Babs returned, it was barely a remnant of what it had been. Mother had gotten tired of Daddy not appreciating everything she did for him and wanted to force a crisis where he would realize her value to him. But her leaving him had backfired on her when he turned not to her but to a paramour he had been seeing on the side.

This was a big shock to Babs, as Daddy always seemed to have been loyal to Mother, he was the rock who provided stability.

And it threw Mother into an emotional spin.

With her older sisters Marilyn Jo and Dana both married and moved out of state, now home just consisted of a bitter older woman and her younger daughter who had always been a Daddy's girl and was hurt when he made her stay behind. When they yelled at each other, which was constantly,

Babs could see that they were arguing at cross purposes. Wanting to make peace, she approached her sister, "Janet, what Mother is trying to get across to you is …"

"No, Babs, you're just on her side!"

So, she approached her mother, expecting a more mature response: "Mother, what Janet is trying to say to you is …"

"Well, you're just on her side!"

This was getting her nowhere! So, Babs decided to be the responsible one, and got a job at the neighborhood Hardy's. Janet was still finishing high school, and Mother had a job downtown. All three women pretty much lived their own lives. When Janet had her friends over while Mother was on a date, Babs made herself useful by buying the beer for them. And then got herself in hot water when Mother came home unexpectedly and caught Babs in her "sacred bed" with one of Janet's friends! She still couldn't help herself!

But then Mother's tongue-lashing ended up with, "Okay, Babs, since you're of age, why don't you bar-hop with me instead of hanging around with those kids?" Wow, Mother was sure going through a deep trough since Daddy remarried.

"Sounds good to me, Mother. We can go downtown to some ritzy hotel bar and see who we can meet there. Maybe we can hook up with some rich guys."

So, they both dressed up and went out hunting for worthy dates.

"Hello, ladies, can we buy you a drink?

Schuyler was a businessman from Europe, and he had the most charming accent! He said his business was in Poiesti, just north of Bucharest the capital of Romania. Not that she would be familiar with the location! She'd never even been outside the good ole' US of A, except that time she drove over the Canadian border on that dirt road while she was dancing in North Dakota!

Mother complained that Babs got the handsome one, while she got stuck with the one who didn't even know English! But they both had a good time that night, and Schuyler got Babs' phone number.

Schuyler took Babs to the nicest, most expensive places on their dates. Mother thought he was taking her "down the road" but Babs was having the time of her life. The only thing, even coming home didn't provide any outside pressure any more to help her live a morally better life. She had been taught since childhood that God didn't approve of sex outside of marriage, but she still kept falling into bed with every guy she liked, and she tended to like guys!

Then came a Saturday when Babs found herself home alone while Mother and Janet were out doing their own things, and Babs got to thinking about what to do with her life. Here she was back at the hub of the wheel. She could go in any direction she wanted. She could marry Schuyler and let him take her across the world—if he would marry her. But doing that might just put her into his cage. She could go back to school and take classes to do something important with her life. What did she want to do? What would make her happy?

Had she ever really been happy? There was that time in high school when the counsellor asked her if she was happy, knowing of her dysfunctional home, and her answer had been, "Well, I'm contented."

The priest had pounded on his desk and said, "Cows are contented—be happy!" That was when the Dairy commercials pronounced that their milk came from "contented cows!"

At least she was contented back then. What did she have? She had religion. But religion by itself hadn't done it, it couldn't help her clean up her act. But maybe God had something to do with it?

At that moment, God showed up! He pulled out of the back of her mind something she'd recently read in a Life Magazine. These were the days when the students were burning their campuses; but these students on the cover were the anomaly, they were smiling and riding on each other's shoulders. One of them had been quoted as saying, "All you need is Jesus!" So, God whispered to Babs, "All you need is Jesus." Then, "All you need is JESUS!" Then, "ALL YOU NEED IS JESUS! Over and over.

Okay. Babs recalled everything she'd been taught about Jesus: He was true God and true man; born of a virgin; lived a perfect, sinless life; died for the sins of the world; rose from the dead; and physically ascended into Heaven. She had never doubted any of that before, but there was something different now.

When she'd thought of His dying before, she always considered how many people there are in the world, and every person has a lifetime of sins; so no wonder He had to suffer that much, to allot a little for every sin committed.

That's when God showed her Jesus on the Cross, and she realized that she deserved that execution, He didn't, and He did it for her; He took her place on that Cross as though she were the only one! And that was how much God loved her!

Oh. my. gosh! Nobody had ever loved her like that before! Why would God love her after all she'd done against Him and His ways? She only deserved execution, not this welcoming she felt! She wept!

Then she thought about what had brought her to this moment: she didn't know how to live her life! God was right there, so she talked to Him for the first time—not a "prayer"—just talking to Him. She said, "God, I don't know how to live my life. I know that You made this life You gave me, and You know why You made it, I don't. And every time I try to live it, I mess it up. So, I don't even want to try to live it anymore; if You want this life to be lived, You'll have to live it, because I refuse to!"

She heard herself talking to God this way, and halfway expected lightening from the ceiling! But God just smiled, and He took over her life that day.

She walked out of that room floating, she felt so light! God had taken her heavy burden of sin off of her shoulders and placed it on Jesus at that moment in time. And when she thought about all those "truth systems" she'd been investigating, that she found so interesting, she now realized why none of the occult or paranormal beliefs actually convinced her—she could see now that each one wove in a little or more than a little deception!

When Schuyler came over that night, she told him that they could be just friends, because she wasn't going to sleep with him anymore.

"But why? What happened to you, Babs, honey?"

She really couldn't say exactly what had happened, so she just said, "I gave myself to God today, and I don't have to do that stuff anymore."

"Don't have to? You never had to!"

"You're right, everything I did was because I chose to do it; but I have another choice now, I can choose to do right, and not fall into that sin anymore!" Babs learned later that when she admitted to God that she deserved death and let Jesus take her place on the Cross, then His blood washed her so clean that His Holy Spirit came into her spirit, and cut off the connection between the new spiritual life and the human flesh that was sinful, and that broke her addiction instantly.

"So, you're not going to sleep with me tonight?

"No. If that's all you want from me, then you can go home now."

"Well, if that's how you're going to be, then I'm out of here! This is ridiculous! You'll get over it, they always do! Call me when you come to your senses!"

Babs didn't even miss him. It was crazy, but it seemed like she saw everything different now. Nothing around her had changed, but it was like she had new eyes to see much more than she ever had before.

She didn't even need to have a boyfriend anymore. All the fun she was having with them was empty, anyway; now she had the joy of the Lord, a happiness she didn't even understand! And finally she was free! But she was just a newborn baby, and she had a lot to learn.

CHAPTER 6

Trying to Live in the Light

"Babs, what kind of cards are these? What card game do you play with them?"

"Mother, those are Tarot cards. You don't use them for card games, they tell fortunes."

"Fortunes? Do they work?"

"Well, yeah, they're supposed to."

"Can you tell me how my relationship will go with my new boyfriend Hugh?"

"I don't know a lot about how to interpret each card, but I can tell the general direction they're pointing to."

"Hmm, let me see. This card doesn't look too good, oh, well, this one looks pretty bad, too, mmm. All I can tell with this layout is that your relationship may hit some rocky spots, but everything will work out all right at the end. I don't know enough about the cards to give you any details."

"Well, that's not what I wanted to hear, but I hope it does work out in the end."

"Who is this guy, Mother? The one who went off his meds and threw you down the stairs?"

"Oh, Babs, he's a really nice guy when he's himself. I heard of a new wonder-drug for manic-depression and I'm getting him into a testing program for it. If I can fix him up, I'll marry him, and he'll take care of me."

"But if he doesn't stay on the meds he has now because he doesn't want a doctor to run his life, do you think he'll agree to you running his life?"

"I won't be running his life! But when he sees how good he feels on this new drug, Lithium, he'll want to stay on it."

"If you say so!"

"Well, I've arranged to have him enrolled in this drug trial at the hospital laboratory downtown, so he will be over tonight for me to take him down there."

"You're taking your car, not his?"

"Hugh lost his driver's license, so a friend will be bringing him over. So, we'll take my car, you can't use it tonight."

"That's fine, I'm not planning on going anywhere, anyway.

Babs wasn't interested in bar-hopping any more, she was perfectly contented to read. So, she settled down on the couch with a good book.

Meanwhile, Hugh was thinking he didn't want this woman telling him what to do either, so he had his friend take him to every hospital in the whole metro area, thinking that if he was already in a hospital, he wouldn't have to go to hers. But every other hospital refused to take him, because he'd already signed himself in previously and walked out. And they also visited friends along the way. All day.

So, when they finally got to their house, the friend came in with him, thinking they were just going to visit for a few minutes. When Hugh left with Mother, the friend stayed—he saw Babs on the couch, and she had long hair and wasn't wearing a bra! He was in love at first sight! (Or was it lust at first sight?)

This friend was a big guy, over six feet tall, and he seemed to be interested in Babs, so she thought she'd freak him out by confronting him with her Ouija board; it hadn't worked for her since she "gave herself to God." She would learn later that now that God's Spirit was in her, the demon of the board couldn't use her body to move the planchette.

"Oh, you've got one of those! My mom has one, too, it's a lot of fun when relatives come over. The spirit of her board is Ahab."

"Well, this one doesn't work anymore."

"Really? Let's try it …".

"It seems to be answering our questions." Because he was moving the planchette to point to what he wanted it to say! But he wouldn't admit this until years later.

"But it's lying, it's not telling us the truth." Because he didn't know her yet.

"Why do you say that?"

"Because I'm not going to marry you—I'm not going to marry anybody! I'm already married!"

"Already married? Where's your husband?"

"Oh, I left him, he's out of state. And I don't need anyone, anyway.

"Well, you seem to be someone I'd like to get to know. Can I come over tomorrow after work? It's Halloween, I'll take you out for the holiday!"

Steve came by again the next night, and took her to Sir Robin's Den, a tiny dance-hall-bar out on the highway. But he wouldn't dance with her! He said he didn't know how. And here she was, a former professional dancer!

He kept coming over every night after work, as he worked in her neighborhood at a friend's welding shop. Sometimes he took her over to his parents' house to shower and change when they went out, so she met his family. And he had a little sister that just didn't look or act normal to Babs.

As they drove together to the restaurant, she asked, "Steve, what's wrong with your little sister?" and she looked down, not knowing what kind of answer he will give. And he was quiet! Was he angry that she'd asked, and drew attention to the child, who obviously wasn't normal? She'd thought that because the family had acted normal when she obviously wasn't, there were two possibilities. Either they were ignoring her differences, or they had accepted her and were taking proper steps to care for her. But he was quiet.

Finally, he said, "I'm sorry I didn't prepare you. Sandie has Downs Syndrome. It's sometimes called being Mongoloid because of their slanted eyes, but that's a misnomer. She was my mom's change-of-life baby, and the condition is caused by an extra chromosome. She's been in special schools and she'll never grow older than about 4 years old mentally. I hope that's all right with you."

Whew! Babs had heard about Downs Syndrome, but never saw one in person before. But this family must accept this special child so completely as a family member that Steve didn't even think to "prepare" her before bringing her to meet his family. And they were taking care of her needs appropriately. Babs was impressed and respected this greatly.

When they were hanging out with his friends, they were usually in a garage or a bachelor pad full of beer cans. Steve seemed to have a cigarette and a can of beer in his hands all the time. And his friends would make comments, like, "Boy this girl must be really something, Steve, you haven't used any "language" all afternoon!"

What was really different for Babs was that they weren't sleeping together, just hanging out days and going out nights, but not spending overnights together. Since she considered that God was steering her life now, she assumed that He had brought Steve into her mother's living room that night; so, she passively went along with what must be God's plan for her. And she was really getting to like this guy.

She got the impression that Steve must be a jack of all trades but a master of none; but the better she got to know him, she realized that he seemed to be master of them all! She admired his high intelligence, and that he could figure out how to solve any kind of problem. And it seemed that whatever he wanted to do; he'd do it himself, and he could figure out how to do it well.

Steve kept telling her he loved her, and that he wanted her to marry him; and Babs realized that this relationship was based on more of a friendship than a physical relationship, like all her other boyfriends. Maybe she was even coming to love him. But she insisted that his family lawyer get her a divorce from Tom (since he never did divorce her) before she would agree to be officially engaged. So he did.

On Christmas Eve he gave her an engagement ring.

CHAPTER 7

Living in a Little More Light

Babs married Steven Theo Watson at an actual church wedding that next spring. Since she didn't have a church and he did, she had been going with him. They talked with his Lutheran minister and arranged to use the beautiful little chapel off of the main auditorium, since she'd been married before. They'd both been honest with each other about their pasts. Babs didn't want to hurt Steve like Tom had hurt her in not being honest from the start.

The reception was at her new in-law's house where he'd been living, and while she was unwrapping the wedding presents in the living room, the guys were all out front cheering him on as he showed off on his new drag bike he'd built. Suddenly they all came barreling in looking for water and bandages to take care of his road-rash, but Steve's interest was to first see if his bike was damaged. This set the tone to color their first summer together.

Now that he'd bagged his quarry and made Babs his wife over the fall, winter and spring, Steve was now free to use his spare time in pursuing his great love: motorcycle drag-racing at the racetrack.

She learned that Steve had been fabricating his own motorcycles since he was in junior high, building little miniature motorcycles and winning ribbons for them at the local car shows. He had all the pics and trophies to prove his achievements. Babs was new to this sport, but she enjoyed watching him, and felt proud of him when the grandstand showed their approval. He only rode on the drag strip, not having a street bike until years later, but he offered to build Babs her own race-bike, which she declined.

In his drive to be the best, Steve had become a master welder working at his friend's welding shop, and a year after their wedding he opened his own welding business doing work on the motorcycles of the biker groups in town. And whenever the national racecar drivers were in town and needed welding on their sling-cars, they came to him, too, knowing, his work from the shop he worked at when they met.

Now that they were married he felt that he didn't have to be on his "best behavior" anymore, and Babs learned the extent of Steve's big three bad habits. Number one was his mouth; he never let three words out of his mouth that two of them were unrepeatable. Number two was his smoking; he went through at least a whole pack of cigarettes each day. And number three was his beer. She noticed while they were dating that he always had a beer in his hand, now she realized it was a new can every 20 minutes or so, because he consumed a case every day. When he woke up each morning, he had to imbibe of "the hair of the dog" and start a new day of beer drinking.

Eventually Babs learned that Steve had to be the expert in whatever he did, and if he couldn't be the best at it, he didn't need to fool with it. Like he had no use for sports because he was not that well-coordinated. He always had a half-dozen irons in the fire at any one time, though, following the adage of "If it is to be, it is up to me!"

His favorite hobby was motorcycle drag racing at the drag strip most week-ends. Since Steve worked for himself, he could spend the whole day bench-racing with his motorcycle friends, then when they went home to their families, he would get to work on the work he had to do. So, he never wanted to eat supper before ten o'clock at night, because after eating he wanted to sleep.

Babs was still working downtown, now doing bookkeeping for a company who manufactured eyeglasses and she needed to be up early to get to the office on time, so, she took a nap when she got home from work. When Steve came in after he finished his work, she'd fix supper.

One night at supper, he had news. "Guess what, Babs, one of the big Top Fuel racers, Big Daddy Don Garlits, was in town today for the races, and brought his car in for me to weld, and, Baby, he offered me a job building his cars for him down in Florida! And he's going to pay me a lot more than we're making now, and the cost of living is a lot less there."

"Would we be moving to Florida?"

Steve really wanted to do this because he knew he drank too much beer. The drunk's dream is to move away from all those other guys who make him drink! And that's how Steve was thinking.

So, Babs put in her two weeks' notice and Steve bought a tractor-trailer rig to pack both his shop and their household furniture into and they took off for Florida, Babs driving the car following Steve in the truck. What an experience!

When they got there, Don let them live "out on the farm," his original homestead house about a half-mile out of the little town of Seffner, and Steve would drive into Tampa to work for him. The post office didn't deliver out that direction, so Babs kept fit by walking the half mile to the post office box and back every day to get the mail.

Soon they moved into a brand-new mobile home on Bullfrog Creek, with the landlady's trailer a little further up the path across the creek. Beyond that was her son's trailer.

Since no one had lived in this trailer before them, it seemed that almost every day Babs found something that didn't work right in her new home, so she'd tell her landlady, and she would send her son Paul over after work to fix it. He got home about an hour or so before Steve did, and that's when he'd come over. Since Babs was friendly, she liked to talk to people, so they conversed while he worked on whatever needed to be fixed.

Now, since Babs knew that she belonged to God, and she knew that the Bible was supposed to be God's word, she remembered reading it before, and bogging down. So, she had concluded that she needed someone to teach her how to read it. A mentor.

She had a "test question" that she would ask someone she thought could help her, but no one had given her a "right" answer yet. She had thought Steve's Lutheran pastor might be God's choice to teach her, so one Sunday after the adult class, she stayed after and asked him, "After Jesus was born, did Mary and Joseph have other children?" This is how God used that conversation she'd had so long ago with her former mother-in-law. She had planted that seed in Babs' mind for God to bring it out now. The minister knew she had been Catholic, so he said, "You can believe what you want about that." She knew that there was an historical truth whether Jesus had siblings or not, so that was a wrong answer, he was not the one God wanted to be her mentor.

Then there was the guy at work. He was an outside salesman who only came into the home office from time to time, and Babs didn't like him. He was big and loud and the way he looked at her made her uncomfortable, like she had no clothes on. When she got home after work one day that he was there, she talked to God about him. She said, "God, I don't like that guy. I know that you love everybody, and I don't want to dislike someone You love, so would You show me something about him that I can like?"

The next time he was in the home office, he was still big and loud, but he was saying stuff like, "Hallelujah!" and, "Praise the Lord!" This was certainly different! And he was talking about going to meetings where they were, "singing the psalms again!" He must have found God!

So, Babs thought maybe she could learn from someone at one of his meetings, so she asked him if he could find the answer to her question. When she asked him, his answer was just a shake of his shoulders. "Well, can you find the answer? Is it in the Bible?" "I don't know!" He seemed to only be interested in verses that talked about drinking poison and handling poisonous snakes.

Now Paul is saying that his brother is a pastor, so while he was wrenching on the bathroom faucet to fix a drip, Babs asked him her question. He stopped wrenching and looked at her, and she could see the wheels turning in his brain, "Should I tell her what I think she wants to know, or the truth?"

He sighed and took the plunge: "Jesus had four brothers and some sisters."

"How do you know that? Is it in the Bible?"

"Yes, it's in the Bible."

Babs was so excited, she practically jumped on him! "Would you show me?"

"Okay, hold on, let me finish this faucet first, then we can sit at the kitchen table and I'll show you in the Bible." And he turned to Matthew 13: 55-56, "Is this not the carpenter's son? Is not His mother called Mary, and his brothers, James and Joseph and Simon and Judas? And His sisters, are they not all with us?" So, finally, she got the "right" answer! This man must be God's choice to teach her about how to read the Bible.

Paul kept on coming over after work to show Babs some other things the Bible talked about, like about Baptism being an acted-out picture of what has already happened spiritually in someone's life, and to show her how to read the Bible. And Babs' attitude went from passively going along with God for the ride, to actively seeking to do what God would want her to do.

CHAPTER 8

The Light's Rocky Road

All of a sudden, Babs couldn't talk to Steve about anything spiritual! If she even mentioned the Bible or God or Jesus, he would explode!

"I don't understand, Paul. I can't mention anything about God to Steve. What's going on?"

"It sounds like Steve is under conviction."

"'Under conviction'? What's that?"

"Never mind, Babs, just keep on doing what you're doing." She didn't learn what that meant until months later under different circumstances.

"What's the matter, Steve? What's your problem? Paul has been teaching me stuff, and I just want to share with you."

"Well, I don't trust that Paul! He sneaks into my house to see my wife when I'm not even there! You know his wife left him the day we moved in, and I think he's trying to use the Bible to worm his way in to taking you away from me!"

"That's ridiculous, Steve, but if you want, I'll tell him not to come over anymore unless you're here, too!"

But she still felt like she was walking on eggshells around him.

Paul had told her that he had recently quit drinking, and his wife had been boo-hooing at church how hard it was to live with a drunk, and when he sobered up, she didn't have anything to complain about to get sympathy anymore, so she left him.

That year, New Year's Eve fell on a Sunday. They usually went to church on Sundays to his Lutheran church which was in another town since they moved. Steve was up early, as usual, fooling around in the trailer of his truck, which he'd set up as a welding shop. The back of the trailer opened to the kitchen window, so he could call out, "Baby, bring me another beer!" and she would comply.

So, when she got up that morning, she called to him out the window, "Are we going to church this morning?"

"Yes, go ahead and get ready, I'll be in in a little bit."

"Okay. Now I'm almost ready, are you coming in?"

"Yeah, I'll be there in a minute."

"We have to leave in ten minutes, are you going to get dressed?"

"Yeah."

But he still didn't come inside to dress for church.

So, she walked out to his trailer.

"Well, it's time to leave and you're not dressed. You're not going, are you?"

"No, not this morning."

"Well, I'm all ready to go!"

"Then go ahead!"

"But you know I don't like going by myself!"

"Then don't go."

"But I'm all dressed for church!"

"Then go."

"I don't even think I know how to get there without you!"

"Steve, Paul said we could go with him, I just saw him going to his car, is it okay if I go with him?"

Exasperated, Steve told her, "Do whatever you think is right!"

She would've expected him to say, "whatever you want," but he said, "whatever is right!"

"Well, it's right to go to church on Sunday, so, thank you, I'll go with Paul. See you later!"

Paul was just coming down the drive as Babs approached him, so he stopped and hopped out of the car. She asked, "Can I go to church with you?"

"Sure, uh, is Steve coming, too?"

"No, just me."

"Is it okay with him for you to come with me?"

"Sure, he told me to do what was right, so I'm going to church."

This was the first time Babs had gone to a church that wasn't a "high church" of a major denomination, and there wasn't any "ceremony" about this service. It was a tiny church building, and there were barely a dozen people there, and she seemed to be the only "guest." Then a man came out and started to lead the congregation in singing. In her experience, the only time the congregation sang was when the priest was late to start the mass! So, she whispered to Paul, "When will the service start?"

He replied, "This is the service!"

After the sermon, the congregation was led to sing, "Just As I Am," all five verses, waiting for someone to "come forward." Since Babs was the only stranger there, she figured they were waiting on her, so she got up and approached the preacher, and told him that she needed baptism.

Paul was grinning from ear-to-ear, thinking that she had just gotten saved!

On the way out of that little church building, she shook the preacher's hand, and said, "Pray for my husband, I don't think he's a Christian yet."

When she got home, there was a small crowd of neighbors out front at their pump, so she went in and changed out of her church clothes. As she was heading back out the door, Steve was charging in: "Where do you think you're going?"

"Out to the party at the pump!"

"Come here, I need to talk to you!"

"I don't know what you think you're doing, running off alone with that guy! You know I don't trust him! He could have taken you out to some orange grove and raped you! And with your past, you wouldn't have a case against him!"

"But he took me to church!"

Then Steve went into a tirade! "Yeah, and I'm working my fingers to the bone to try to earn enough money to buy you things, and you go running off to church!" Steve was working for Garlits at his factory in Tampa, and also working in his trailer as a workshop.

She couldn't help herself; she finally had to quote a bible verse to him: "Seek first the kingdom of God, and all these things will be given to you also!"

And he headed out the door and took off in his truck!

She didn't know if she'd ever see him again!

She'd chased him off!

The guy she loved and was actually faithful to!

What would she do now?

Later that afternoon Steve was quietly back in his workshop.

Then there was a knock on her front door. "Hi, I'm your neighbor down road. I saw you at church this morning, and I wanted to invite you to our watch-night service tonight for New Years, to pray in the New Year. We're having the regular evening service, then a Gospel group is coming down the coast from an evening service in Sarasota, so we're having a social out on the patio until they come for the watch-night service. Would you like to come?"

"Yes, I'd like to come, but not unless Steve comes with me."

"Oh, let's ask him."

"No, that's okay, I'll approach him with the invite. Thank you."

"Steve, that was our neighbor up the road. She wanted to (invite us to church tonight,) wasn't that nice of her to think of us and come all the way down the road?

"Yeah, nice lady."

Babs fixed Sunday dinner, and asked Steve what he wanted to do to celebrate the New Year.

"I don't know, do you have anything in mind?"

"Well, I don't want to go bar-hopping, with all the drunks out driving; and we didn't know anyone having a New Year's party." She offered, "Some of the churches are having meetings, can we go to one of those?"

"Here's the Sunday paper church section, see anything there you want to go to?"

"There's a few here, but I don't know any of these churches. That one I went to this morning is having a service, do you want to go there?" Babs really did want to go back to that little church she went to that morning with Paul, and their neighbor even came by to invite them.

"Well, okay, but I'll have to change clothes. What time does it start?"

She checked the clock, and said, "Pretty soon, we'll have to leave right away."

So they threw their better clothes on and drove to the church.

"Here we are, oh, we're not late, they're still out on the patio. Let's join them."

Steve immediately found the pastor and breathed his beery breath in his face: "H-h-hello, Pastor!" to get his reaction. If this pastor was offended by his beer-breath, then he could discount whatever he would be saying to him as being hypocritical.

"Oh, hello there, so glad you could join us tonight!"

And that pastor wasn't fazed at all and didn't even flinch.

And someone said, "Oh, here's the Gospel group, we can all go in now."

Steve and Babs let everyone else go first and followed behind them into the little building. They ended up in the last pew on the left, Steve, then Babs, then their neighbors. The building was packed, not a seat left in the whole church. During the service, the lead guitar guy in the gospel group would strum, cry, and say, "Thank God I'm saved!" At one point, they had people in the pews stand and testify, "I thank God He healed me!" "Praise God He brought my prodigal child home!" "Thank God for His great grace to me!"

Steve was amazed that all these people were in a church instead of out partying on New Year's Eve night. And nobody cared that this guy was actually crying! And all the joy on all their faces, he'd never felt anything like what they were showing.

Then when it was close to midnight, the pastor invited whoever wanted to come down to the altar and pray the New Year in. Babs wanted to go down front, so she motioned to Steve to let her out of the pew, and he stepped out. But instead of stepping back to let her out, he headed forward, too. She followed him down the outside aisle to the step and they both knelt down.

The pastor saw them, and scooted around to kneel beside Steve, and they were whispering! Babs couldn't hear what they were saying!

When they finally got home after it all, Babs asked Steve what he'd talked about with the preacher, and he told her how much he'd been impressed with the people there, and had asked the pastor how they could be so happy. The pastor had told him how Jesus died for each of us to save us, and he told him to let Jesus take his place on the cross.

"So, did you?"

"What do you think?" and he grinned at her.

She just figured that she'd see how this would work out, and they went to bed.

Since the next day was New Year's Day, Steve was home from work for the holiday, and fiddled all day in his workshop. Babs noticed, though, that things must not have been going very well, because she kept hearing him say, "Oh, shoot!" "Darn it!" "Drat!" This was new, he'd never used substitute words before!

Next morning, as he was leaving for work, he told Babs that he thought he was going to quit drinking beer!

"That's good, honey." She'd heard this before. "Is there any beer in the 'fridge?"

"I think there's two or three cans."

"What should I do with them?"

"Why don't you throw them away."

"Are you sure? You don't want to keep them just in case?"

"No, throw them out!"

And he went off to work with a swagger!

And Babs had a blast pouring those beers down the drain!

One day during that first week of the year, Steve came barreling in the door, flung his pack of cigarettes on the couch, and declared, "If my smoking cigarettes will keep even one person out of Heaven, then I'll never smoke another cigarette!" and charged back out! Well, what was that about? He must have been talking to someone about being a Christian, with a cigarette in his hand, and the other person used that as an excuse to not listen to him about the Lord. Steve never did smoke another cigarette again!

So, his "big three" were now history! God had worked a miracle in him, and it was obvious to everyone! God had put His Spirit into Steve, which gave him the new ability to turn his back on all three of these bad habits that had plagued him. Even Don Garlits noticed his complete turn-around.

But it wasn't so great for Babs.

"Why is this place always a mess, Babs?"

"My lack of housekeeping never bothered you before!"

"Well before I was cussing and drinking and smoking. Now I want you to clean up this dump!"

Oh no! Now that Steve was a Christian, Babs was going to have problems!

CHAPTER 9

Baby Steps

Babs had requested Baptism that morning she first attended that little church, having learned from Paul that Christian Baptism is a picture of what had already happened. And from what Paul showed her those afternoons at the kitchen table, she knew that she had become a Christian that Saturday in Mother's house, when God had showed her Jesus on the Cross and she'd admitted that she deserved it and that He had taken her death. That's when God had washed her in the blood Jesus shed, and put His Holy Spirit into her spirit, giving her the ability to take the new, better choices she had made since then.

So, she had asked for Baptism, understanding that this would be the next step. Now that Steve had also become a Christian, they decided to be Baptized together, and they made the arrangements with the pastor of that little Baptist church.

Paul was excited for them and asked to invite his brother and his wife, Shell and Char, to the Baptism, too, and Babs impulsively invited them all over for a light supper after. When they got to their trailer, Babs said she wanted to make Hot Dog and Potato Soup for them all, and showed Char her biggest pot, which was not nearly big enough for all of them! So, they borrowed a bigger pot, and all enjoyed the soup together.

That's how they met Shell and Char. He was an ordained Southern Baptist minister, and while they ate the soup together he told them about having had a youth home up in New York State. He missed working with the young people, and said he wanted to have something similar down here in Tampa and was looking for a young couple to be house-parents.

After everyone left, they talked about this opportunity. Babs was all for it, but Steve said he'd have to talk to Shell about it some more before he could decide whether to take that responsibility.

About a week later Shell and Char found a little church in town that only had a few people attending it, and the present pastor there was looking to move on. So, over the next couple weeks Shell and Char and their three daughters, and Paul, and Steve and Babs all joined the little church, swelling its membership roll.

Then a month later when the other pastor announced his departure to go to a different church, the membership all voted to install Shell as its new pastor. Now they had a big church building with a

Sunday school building to house their new ministry, Soul Patrol for Christ.

While Steve was discussing with Shell the requirements they would be expected to meet, they agreed that Shell and Paul and Steve would all retain their day jobs to support the home while the ladies mothered the boys.

Babs overheard Shell telling Steve that they had been criticized in New York for "seducing young men into accepting Christ with the girls' sexy clothing," so they had to require the girls to lower the hems on their mini-skirts to brush the sidewalk when they kneeled to pray with other teens on the street.

Babs looked at her own clothing, and all of her skirts and dresses were still super short, and she thought street-witnessing would be fun! So, she re-sewed the hem in the one dress she had that she hadn't cut off yet and wore it to church on Sunday. After church, she asked Char if she had any dresses Babs could wear, because this was her only dress. Char answered that she'd seen her in several other dresses. "But they're all too short!"

"What do you mean, they're too short? You've been wearing them!"

"But it's more modest to wear them at mid-knee, like this one.

"Who told you to change the way you dress?"

"No one. I overheard Steve and Shell talking and I decided it was time I dressed more like what a Christian should wear."

"Did they tell you that?"

"No. They didn't even know I could hear them. But I know God wants me to be more modest in my clothing." God had used that overheard conversation to change Babs' attitude toward how she dressed. This is not the first time God changed her, and it wouldn't be the last. And Babs got confirmation later that this was God "speaking" to her, when she found First Timothy 2: 9 where Paul instructs Pastor Timothy to teach the ladies to wear "modest apparel."

Babs and Steve moved into one of the former classrooms, and they tore out some of the interior walls to make dormitories for the boys, from four to six boys in each of the four dorms. Steve built bunk beds for them to all fit into the accommodations the Sunday school building provided. And Shell and Char moved into the two large rooms of the church building basement with their daughters.

Their time at the boys' home was a real learning experience for Babs. She learned how to cook for a crowd instead of just a family, and she did all the laundry for all the boys they had. She was also learning how to get along with all the different personalities of the boys and Shell and Char.

And while they were there, Babs suffered a miscarriage, that the doctor termed a "missed abortion." She had to explain to the boys that she had not gotten an "induced abortion" which actually kills the baby, but that the medical term "abortion" refers to a baby being "born too soon," and hers had been "missed" because the baby died on its own, but wasn't "born," and needed to be removed. This kind of threw Babs and Steve into wondering if they should even have their own children, since they were caring for other parents' children.

Also while they lived in Florida, Babs was encouraged when she learned that Mother had returned to church and cleaned up her life, moving out to Arizona to be near Janet.

After a couple of years they decided to leave Soul Patrol and Florida and move back to St. Louis to be closer to his family, and Babs got her job back at the optician company there doing the accounts receivables for three of their stores.

Steve was also working; and studying at a Bible Institute in the evenings. He noticed the different slants the different English Bible translations presented, and he wanted to know what God was really saying without depending on any man's opinion. He wanted to study in the original languages, the very words that God inspired the Bible to be written in.

Also, about that time, his conversations with his parents prompted them to call in their Lutheran pastor to have a talk with him to "set him straight" about theology. He listened to what this preacher said, and knew it wasn't quite right, but he didn't have the education to refute him. Apparently this pastor didn't understand that Jesus fulfilled the Personal Sacrifice (in Leviticus chapter 1) for each of us as the Lamb of God.

Then during a visit with relatives on the other side of the state, he asked them if they knew of a theological school he could look into; and so they stopped by Calvary Bible College (Calvary University, now) to talk with them and pick up their catalog.

Back home in St. Louis, they discussed the possibilities.

"Babs, I'd like to move to Kansas City and attend Calvary." He really wanted to show up his mom's pastor and set him straight. "What do you think, would you want to go to classes, too?" He'd noticed that his studying Scripture every night was helping him to grow spiritually faster than Babs, who was just reading the Bible and attending church on Sundays and Wednesday evenings.

"Sure, honey, my high school teachers put me in the high track, anyway, and I think I'd enjoy college now, and learn how to study the Bible like you do."

So, they moved to Kansas City and both enrolled to begin degree programs. Since Babs had taken over their checkbook balancing and bill paying, they both had high credit scores and were able to take out the financial loans to pay for their schooling each semester. God used even Steve's bad attitude of wanting to best his mother's minister to get him across the state to where He wanted him to be, at Bible college.

CHAPTER 10

Growing In the Light

Babs enrolled in a course of full-time study and Steve worked at a job and took a lighter load of classes. Since they started their academic careers with the spring semester, they were behind the other students, but that didn't bother Babs. She liked to sit up front center in the classrooms, so she could make a comment to the teacher from time to time. If she sat further back, she'd be talking with another student!

During Missionary Week Babs enjoyed the varied cultures presented by the missionaries from different areas of the world, and was fascinated with the stories of how they interacted with the different views people have.

Between classes Babs would stop by the campus soda shop and made friends with some of the other students. Most of the students came straight from high school, and Babs and Steve had been married for several years by now, so she was a bit older than they were, but she had always looked younger than her age.

One day the girls were complaining about their roommates, and Babs replied, "Yeah, my roommate, he …"

"He? You live off campus?"

"Yes, I'm married, and we have an apartment in town."

"Married? How old are you? . . . O my gosh, you're only a year younger than my mother!"

"Well, now you can see your mother with new eyes!"

The on-campus radio station interviewed Steve and Babs on-air as older married students, to encourage other adults who might consider enrolling.

Steve finally bought a Harley Davidson motorcycle to ride to and from school and work, so Babs could have the car.

Steve and Babs both did well in their studies. Toward the end of her junior year of her 4-year course of study, she realized that she was pregnant again. Since she had miscarried her first child in Florida, she didn't want to take any chances with this one, so she cancelled the post-session canoe trip. She was due to deliver in December, a week before finals were scheduled, and she didn't think it was worth enrolling if she wouldn't be able to take the exams, so she postponed her senior year until some future time.

Steve then began to take a full-time load, and Babs opted to audit some classes, and joined the student wives' association, where she could bring her little daughter, Naomi, for the ladies to squeal over.

At one point, Steve was considering applying to work in Saudi Arabia, working in the American oil fields there as an engineer, and earn the high wages they paid. Babs welcomed this idea, thinking that she might be able to make friends with some of the local ladies there, and do some evangelism as a missionary. But then she learned that the Americans were confined to their own compound, and weren't permitted to intermingle with the Saudis much at all. So that wouldn't work. And Steve soon dropped that idea, preferring to be his own boss as an entrepreneur, and started another business as a used car dealership, even selling some cars to faculty members.

When the campus moved from Kansas City down to the Richards-Gebauer Airbase, Steve and Babs rented one of the duplexes the school had access to, and their son Ezekiel was born while they lived there. Steve graduated *summa cum laude*, with highest honors, in Biblical Languages, and continued to take graduate classes.

Until he had a serious motorcycle accident, when a woman turned left right in front of him; he ended up through her windshield in her front seat! Good thing he was wearing his full-coverage helmet, it probably saved his life. That's when he stopped riding on the street.

Since they couldn't continue living on Calvary's campus when he stopped taking classes, Steve propped up his broken leg on the dash and went looking for somewhere they could live. He found an old farmhouse on acreage outside town, and he agreed to do work on the house for the rent. As a used car dealer as a college student, he had purchased a motor home that had been repossessed by the bank, which he restored to its original condition. The little family were able to live in this in the back yard of the farmhouse that summer while Steve made the house livable, installing bathrooms and a kitchen. They also took the motor home to visit with Babs' Daddy and his new wife, and learned that he had gone to church with her, heard the Gospel preached, and he had accepted Christ as his Savior, and become a Christian, also.

Babs thought this was wonderful, moving out of the city. This was on 200 acres that were planted in corn, with a large yard, and even huge round hay bales lined up behind the shed out back, where the kids could climb and play.

Now they had a whole house to live in, but Steve was still self-employed, and he became a workaholic, leaving early in the morning and not returning until late most nights. Babs felt like a single mom, so she talked to Steve about making Friday nights date-nights. Babs would line up a local teenager to baby-sit so they could have a dinner out, but he would forget it was Friday and schedule a business meeting, or just not be home. It took a whole year for him to get it into his head that Fridays were for Babs. But he did sometimes make the effort to be home to put the kids to bed.

During this time Babs was pregnant again, and she wondered if this marriage was going to make it. The relationship seemed so fragile. Steve seemed to be slipping away, so she told him that if he left, she would just have to go cross-country to stay with her sister Dana until she had this baby and could get a job up East and start over in Maryland. This scared Steve, realizing that he may never see his kids again, or even meet this third one. Their Friday date nights were very helpful in talking through their issues.

Babs considered their marriage worth working on, and when she finally realized that Steve couldn't sit down and relax in the middle of a mess, she finally got serious about her lack of housekeeping skills. She had heard Sandra Felton on the Christian radio station talking about her book: *The Messies Manual*, and promptly got a copy.

The first idea she incorporated was Sandra's "Mount Vernon Method" of taking one room at a time. She'd go around the room putting all the clutter into three boxes, "another room," "give away," or "trash," while dusting and cleaning. Sandra got the idea when she visited George Washington's home, and asked the housekeeping crew there how they kept the rooms clean while hundreds of visitors traipsed through every day.

Babs' first room really de-cluttered and clean was the living room, and she was so overcome with that small victory along with the hormonal changes that came with the birth of her third child, Ruth, that she sat down in it and cried!

It didn't stay clean for long, and she still needed to learn how to not clutter. So, it was a long journey to build habits, such as: "Don't put it down unless it's where it belongs;" and "A place for everything and everything in its place." These two attitudes helped to keep the clutter down.

But it was a constant pressure on her for several years to try to get a handle on the household situation, especially with three growing children.

Steve started another business in the outbuilding on that farm, and finally let Babs do the bookkeeping for him, hiring a local teenager to take care of the kids while she was across the yard in the "office." It was the thirteenth business he had started, and he previously survived financially by sequestering himself for a week-end in April to go through all the slips of paper he'd collected all year to find out if he'd made any money that year, having lived off cash-flow.

Then one day Steve came home with a new proposition.

"Our landlord has a mill building in the next town, he says I can buy it from him for a really low price and move my business there, and I can build a home for ourselves there, too."

So, Steve moved his business in and hired a carpenter and a plumber and an electrician and other specialized craftsmen to build the home he wanted for them there, too. He wanted it done right, so he had to do it himself, or under his personal supervision. They moved into the warehouse part of the building while he built the house in the tall mill part. It took two years to finish the mansion. As he worked from the top down, the three children's' two-story bedrooms with sleeping lofts were finished first, upstairs, then the kitchen, dining room, guest room and living room with two balconies on what would be the main level on the second floor, and the master bedroom was finished last. The ground level contained the offices and other business areas.

It was so different and unusual that the local newspaper ran a story on it, with photos. And it happened that a guy once came into the office, looked around, then turned around and walked back out, and looked at the building again, then came back in, bewildered. It didn't seem to him like that old building would have such a beautiful inside!

Now that she had a "new" house, Babs had a fresh start on keeping it uncluttered, and determined that there would be no unpacked boxes in sight. This helped her a lot in her quest to "keep house."

On Saturdays Steve would corral the kids, now almost teenagers, assigning them specific areas to sweep, mop and scrub before they would be released to hang out with their friends. So, the house would be clean, not just uncluttered.

Babs was already doing the bookkeeping for the company; she now had a beautiful new office to work in, just downstairs. And since she could give him accurate figures anytime he needed them, he was finally able to make the good business decisions to allow the company to grow and prosper.

As time passed, one day Steve fielded a call from a businessman on the island of Trinidad who asked him if the electrical machine they manufactured could help him with his utility bill at his factory. Since Steve had heard about this Caribbean island as a child, he jumped at the opportunity this presented, and said, "I think I will need to look at your machines to determine what you may need."

"Come on down, you may stay at my house as my guest while you assess my electrical needs."

Steve realized that this may be the only time he'd go there, and he wanted Babs to go with him, so they made the arrangements to fly there together for a week.

After flying all day to get all the way down to the southern Caribbean island, Afaz met them at the Port of Spain Airport and he drove them on the "wrong" side of the streets (on the left, due to the British influence) to Chaguanas, passing by residences and tyre stores and other various and sundry buildings. When they stopped to electronically open the gate in the wall around his house, Steve remarked, "Afaz, you have the nicest house in the neighborhood!"

His was a large house compared with the other structures, and he confidently led them upstairs to his home. It was constructed of concrete blocks instead of wood because it was a tropical island where wood would rot, and the living quarters were on the second floor with decorative cut blocks along the upper walls to allow the breezes to cool the rooms. The dining room table held a bowl of chicken and yellow rice, which had been prepared for them to eat after their long trip, then he led them to their guest room.

It was a lovely home, decorated with beautifully calligraphic Arabic quotations from the Koran, and there were bathrooms everywhere, and each one had a bidet, even the half-bath off the kitchen.

Babs met Saffina in the morning at breakfast and had a wonderful conversation with her while Steve and Afaz drove to the factory. Later the girls went shopping, and Babs thought of getting a beautiful sari like Saffina wore, but when she realized that it was basically just a big scarf wrapped around the body, she didn't think she could manage it without taking Saffina home with her to put it on her! So, she bought a colorful caftan instead.

The next morning for breakfast Afaz took them to a roadside stand to buy them "doubles," a chick-pea paste wrapped in a roti, their flatbread. Then he gave them a tour of the island sights, including buying a fresh coconut off the truck, slicing it open with a machete and drinking the milk before using the sliced piece as a scoop to eat the sweet-meat, a real treat.

This was the first of many vacation trips to Trinidad and Tobago, taken two or three times a year for a week at a time, as Steve couldn't be away from the Company longer than that, because he ran the day-to-day business.

Babs found that she loved the international travel and dreamed of someday travelling the world.

CHAPTER 11

Shadows in the Light

The brighter the light, the deeper the shadow falls.

Steve had sold his drag-bike to a friend when the children were small, considering it to be an expensive hobby they couldn't afford. Now that the business was successful, he was able to buy it back, and let the Company sponsor it. It was The Michigan Madman E.J. Potter's Widowmaker motorcycle, named after Pecos Bill's horse, that he'd bought "in a basket" and modified it to fit his large frame. He also featured the bike in some of their advertisements he designed for the regional trade magazines who carried their ads.

He also wrote a tract, a one-page story about, Qualifying for the Big Race, explaining the facts about becoming a Christian using the picture of meeting the qualifications to run in a racing competition. He planned to use his tract doing dragstrip evangelism. His lay-down bikes were always too powerful to compete in any of the categories, so he did bye-runs, a solo trip down the strip producing a quarter-mile of smoke. He reasoned that his dare-devil antic would buy him the right to talk to the crowd about Jesus. Most churches weren't seeking out these crowds to invite to their services.

When he went to the local drag strips, Babs and the kids, now teenagers, would hand out his tract as, "a story about racing," to the fans in the stands, and would often run out, with people asking, "Can I have one, too?" They always expected to find discarded copies after the crowd left but could only find one or two on the ground after.

But Steve considered the Widowmaker to be "old technology," being a couple of decades old. Now he decided to fabricate a new motorcycle, the Freedom, for the freedom found in Christ, incorporating all the latest tech in metallurgy and design and fuel mixtures. He figured that the new would be safer than the old, always a concern since that street accident.

He worked on the new bike for two years in the basement, while running the company upstairs with Babs and their employees. It took him two years to finish it, because he also spent time on Bible study, still researching in the original languages he'd learned in college. He would often share with her his insights, like when God impressed on him that when Paul said that the wife was the "weaker" vessel, he meant that she is more like a delicate china teacup, as compared to his tin coffee cup (I Peter 3: 7). Babs appreciated his sharing with her what God was teaching him. He was her theologian.

And even though he was a big guy, he never started a fight, because he knew the other guy would hit back, and he didn't want to hurt! And through the years he'd learned how to be gracious and negotiate to a win-win conclusion.

Babs had found a Caribbean cruise online that cost much less than expected for a whole week at sea, and asked Steve if he wanted to go: "It'll be so romantic!"

"Not really, baby, I don't want to be stuck on a boat in the middle of the ocean! Why don't you see if one of your lady friends wants to go with you?"

"You'd let me go without you?"

"If you want, I've taken a couple of weekend trips to Trinidad without you."

Babs considered an older lady in her Ladies Bible Study who had talked about taking some group trips before.

"Norma, have you ever taken a cruise?"

"No, but I'd love to sometime."

So, Babs bought the tickets and started to think about what to pack.

"Babs, I've finished this new bike, and the NHRA (the National Hot Rod Association) is sponsoring Bike Week in Florida, so I'm going to take it down there and see how it runs. I'll be staying at Jerry's in Fort Pierce, he's a racer, too, and I expect to see E.J. there, too."

"Will you be gone when I go on my cruise?"

"No, I should be back a week or two before you leave."

"Good, sweetheart, I'll miss you while you're gone. Be careful."

"You know I will, baby, and then I'll have you again for a little while before you leave!"

He drove down there on Tuesday, to be able to run it on the track to get time slips; and to see how it was running. "Oh, Babs, baby, this bike is terrific! It was faster than the old bike ever went, and it's not even running properly. When I get it tuned up, it will really fly!"

He sounded like a little kid with a new toy. Drag racing on his lay-down bike was his most enjoyable activity. He loved going fast, and drag strips had no speed limits!

She didn't expect him home until Sunday night or Monday and was watching a movie with their son Zeke on Saturday afternoon when the phone rang.

"Hello, is this Babs? This is E.J. Steve had an accident on his bike and they've taken him to the hospital. I'll call you back when I know about his condition."

Steve had never had injuries any worse than a little road rash on any of his bikes, but this sounds more serious!

"Turn the movie off, let's pray for Dad!" And they knelt at the couch and prayed together.

The next call was from the hospital in Ft. Pierce. "Mrs. Watson? This is Dr. Laura Scannell at Lawnwood Regional Medical Center. Are you sitting down?" That's when she knew. "Your husband Steve had an accident. He fell off his motorcycle and he hit a tree. He did not survive."

Babs' fears always concerned her children, but if anyone would have asked her what would be the worst thing that could ever happen to her in this world, her answer would have been, "To lose my husband!" This is exactly what happened! Babs went into a daze, and only focused on the next problem that needed to be solved.

"What was a tree doing at the drag strip?"

"He wasn't at the drag strip; he was on a street."

"But it wasn't a street bike, he would not ride it on a street!"

"All I know is that the motorcycle did not hit the tree, he did."

Babs had to know what had happened to her precious Steve! She immediately bought a plane ticket to Florida to investigate.

"Naomi, Zeke, Ruthie; Dad had an accident on the bike, and he, he, … he died!" And they all collapsed into one anothers arms and cried!

"He's dead?" … "But what happened?" … "Oh, nooooo."

"I have to go down there and find out how this happened!"

She landed at Treasure Coast International Airport early on Sunday afternoon, and E.J. and Jerry met her. They offered to take her to where Steve died on the way to Jerry's house. It was in a new industrial park that nothing had been built on yet; a perfect "personal drag strip." The police had lined out and marked it all so E.J. pointed out that Steve had been making runs down the right-hand lane, the favored lane, and E.J. and Jerry had been timing his runs as Steve listened to the engine. Then Steve would make needed adjustments and ride it back to where he'd started, the guys timing him again.

After several runs up and down the street, Steve was going to make one more run, then pack up everything, spend another night at Jerry's, and drive home after church on Sunday. The last thing he did was to go to his truck to get a Study Bible he'd bought for E.J.'s girlfriend, who was a new Christian. He wanted her to have good Bible teaching, and he knew he wouldn't be there for her. He handed it to E.J. and told him to give it to her. That was his last run.

He started close to the center line, then went toward the center of the lane. He had put a very wide tire on the back for traction, that others had told him would make it hard to steer, but he had shown the officials at the drag strip that he could handle it.

This time he kept going right until he was riding in the gutter. Drag strips don't have gutters, and he slowed down to try to get back in the lane. There was a culvert sticking up from the curb, and it caught his right leg, pulling him off the bike. E.J. and Jerry saw him put his arms up in the air right before he went down, and he tumbled head-over-heels in the grass until he struck the tree, square to his chest, breaking all of his ribs and the sternum, too.

E.J. called 911 immediately as Jerry applied CPR until the ambulance arrived. They worked on him for about 40 minutes, and never got a flicker of life out of him.

They pronounced him dead at the hospital.

Now that Babs had seen the circumstances, she called the medical center and talked with Dr. Scannell, who told her, "I'm at the hospital now, when can you come to talk with me about this?"

Jerry agreed to take her immediately, so they went, and Babs sat down with the doctor.

"Understand, I only examined him to determine enough damage to end his life. There may be more injuries internally. I found his right femur broken and extruded, and his sternum was broken, and all of his ribs."

Babs was shaken, but she had to finish this. She needed to see his body, to see for herself where the bruises were, where the dirt smudged, all the details. So, she called the medical examiner's office and asked if she could look at his body.

"I'm sorry, we did the autopsy and sewed him back up, but we don't have a place to separate him from the rest of the bodies, and it wouldn't be safe to let you in."

"Then I'll need to talk to the funeral home here."

"Hello, are you the ones who will prepare my husband's body for transfer to Missouri? I need to see it before he's washed, when can I come see him?"

"Oh, you can't see him until we prepare him, he's had an autopsy, he's wide open!"

"I talked to the doctor who did the autopsy, and he told me he sewed him up. Now tell me when I can see his body."

"We can't let you do that; it would upset you too much!"

"You don't know me or what would upset me!"

"Well, we still won't let you look at him until we wash the body."

"Hello, Atkinson Funeral Home? Michael, can you find someone in Florida to accept my husband's body before it is washed or otherwise prepared? I need to see for myself what this did to him. Please?"

"Yes, I need to see his body as it is, and the home that has him here in Florida won't let me see him."

"Oh, Michael, thank you for calling all those funeral homes in Florida! Yes, I can go down to Miami to see him. Thank you so much!"

Steve's aunt was in Florida visiting her daughter there, and they drove Babs down from Ft. Pierce to Miami. The cousin waited in the car while the aunt went into the round chapel to sit in the ante-area to be available if needed while Babs entered the inner sanctum.

He was not in a box. His body lay there on a slab, covered with plastic.

Babs lifted the sheet and opened the plastic, and there was his body. Totally exposed.

She forced herself to look at where all the bruises and smudge spots were, and they were in all the expected places, as well as in some unexpected places.

All the details she could see as she looked at his empty body did answer some of the questions she had as to what had actually happened to him.

And she was able to talk to him about what in the world she would ever do without him.

And she hugged him and said goodbye! And it was a real closure. She needed that with him, even though she knew he wasn't there anymore.

She walked out of that little chapel deflated.

But there was still another problem to solve. She had to get his ring.

She had just given him a diamond wedding ring as a Christmas present, because he was finally able to wear a ring, without getting it caught in some machine. As the president of his corporation he wasn't working the machines himself anymore. When she'd given it to him, he thought it was too pretentious, so they brought it back to the store to get a more modest style; but comparing it to the other jewelry there he realized that the ring Babs had gotten him already had the smallest stones, so he felt better about wearing it.

He had to have it on his finger for the funeral.

But the city of Fort Pierce had collected all his effects, impounding the bike and everything else, pending an inquiry into what caused the accident. So, Babs sat with the funeral director in Miami and called the Fort Pierce police. Everyone she talked to said, "I understand, but my hands are tied. Maybe my supervisor can help you, here's the number." She worked all the way up to the police chief!

When she called his number, it was almost 5:00, and she expected to get his secretary, but he answered it himself! The secretary had already left. And he understood her dilemma, also. "But don't give me the address, that would imply that I would be able to send it to you. I'll have my secretary call you tomorrow for your address if I can send it. Be looking for her call."

The next morning Babs was on her way back to Missouri, and when she was ready to leave the airport in Kansas City, her phone rang. It was the chief's secretary asking for her address to overnight the ring for his funeral.

Back home in Harrisonville, she spent two full days with Michael, the Funeral Director at Atkinson. He and his assistant were very gracious in leading her through all the details. She enlisted her family and friends to call all the lists of people Steve had in his Rolodex, and all the other lists and stacks of business cards in his desk. It seemed like he knew everybody.

The funeral was on Friday, and the line to enter extended all around the block.

After the funeral and burial, Babs' church ladies had laid out a spread of wonderful foods to serve the crowd in the big party room, and Babs ate at the conference table in her office with all her relatives who came in from across the country. It's a sad state of affairs how someone has to die to get families together.

When Babs went into the main room, she realized that there were people from all over the country that came to honor him, and even Afaz came from Trinidad!

Babs was so grateful to God for not making Steve suffer. When the autopsy report came, it showed that when he struck the tree at about 30-35 miles per hour, it not only broke all the bones in his chest, but it also tore the aorta from his heart. He died instantly. He was taken from what he enjoyed most in this life directly to standing in glory in the next. She could imagine him looking around and asking, "What am I doing here?"

Steve and Babs' thirty-year marriage had been having their best years ever. He died six weeks short of their anniversary.

After all the busyness of the last two weeks, Babs thought about that cruise she had bought into, and wondered if she should go after all. She had a business to run, and she needed to learn how. But it was a non-refundable ticket, and she had to get away to clear her head and figure it all out.

So, she went with Norma on a Carnival Cruise to the Caribbean.

CHAPTER 12

Out of the Deep Shadow

Norma had been a counsellor to the bereaved, a surprise to Babs. Going on that cruise was the best thing she could have done at that time, like God had planned it all along. They offered a 2 for 1 deal on a full body massage, so they both signed up at half price, the first night aboard. This helped Babs relax, to be able enjoy the rest of the cruise.

They stayed busy every day, opting for shore excursions on the islands they visited each day, snorkeling, taking tours, going on hikes; or just spending a day shopping, sampling the cuisine for lunch on the islands and returning to the ship for the evening shows and other entertainments. They would sail overnight to a new island each day, and the only day aboard ship was the last day, when they sailed from Barbados back to San Juan all night and day, which Babs used to assess how she was going to reorganize her employees to run the Company her way. She lounged on the deck with her clipboard and pencil, and re-structured the order of authority, penning a letter to all those in her employ delineating the responsibilities accorded to each one.

This was new for her, as Steve had always managed the employees as well as handling the day to day activities in a very hands-on way, and Babs only did the bookkeeping, including the Payables and Payroll and EOMs and EOQs and Year End. Steve's secretary, Cate, had been his right hand with the customers, guiding them to which of our converters would best run their machines, and she also handled the Receivables.

Cate had taken his death really hard and was telling prospective customers that the Company had closed! So, Babs had everyone else answering the phone instead of her, not able to trust her anymore. So she quit.

Losing a key employee like Cate as well as the Founder and President of the company kind of put the death knell on the business. Babs had never run a company before, and for two years they lost money.

When Babs learned from their insurance guy that he knew a couple of brothers who were an engineer and a business management guy that wanted to buy the Company, Babs knew that these brothers combined the qualities Steve had to be able to run the company as he had.

So she found a business-selling realtor and hired them to handle the transaction, and they gave her a deep discount for already finding the buyer.

She was able to help craft a contract that would continue to pay her the dividend on the patent Steve had on the specialized part used in the machines that made them the best in the industry.

But then the new owners cancelled all the ads in all the trade papers where all the sales came from, thinking that they were too expensive, so they ended up selling so few of the machines that they had to add other products to fill in, and Babs lost out in that deal. But the sale price she received paid off all the debts and she lived on the proceeds for several years.

Two years after the funeral, Babs was still struggling to get out of the deep grief she was experiencing in losing her life-mate. Her children were growing up, and they were concerned for their mom. They wanted her to get medical attention to see what could help with her depression, but all Babs heard was, "Mom, you need to go to a doctor you can't afford to get on drugs you don't want to take"!

About that time her church was beginning a new ministry, Celebrate Recovery, for people with addictions. She was avoiding an addiction to any drugs a doctor would prescribe, but she went to the meetings anyway to see if they could help her deal with her grief.

She signed up for a focus group of just a few women who would be honest and accountable to one another. Then she started to wade through the materials: "What are you able to control?" Whatever her answer to that would be, would not be true—we only have control of our own thoughts and actions. We are responsible only for these, that we often blame others for. She was surprised to learn that we tend to think we can control what we can't, and what we can control, we shirk the responsibility for.

This was her first step out of that deep shadow. Continuing to work through the twelve steps helped her to realize how much she had depended on Steve, and how to learn to take responsibility for herself. She felt like an onion, that over and over every layer she peeled off revealed another layer, another problem connected to another area of life she also needed to work through.

She thought, "Now I'll have to finally grow up!" Interesting that when she reached her 50's she realized this. Steve had spoiled and pampered her, now she will have to face the cold world without him. Was there anyone she could turn to for help?

Babs thought of that verse, "When my father and my mother forsake me, then the Lord will take me up" (Psalm 27: 10). She felt forsaken, so for the first time in her life, she started to read Scripture every day, having a morning "quiet time" with the Lord. Whenever she had tried to set aside a regular time before, it didn't work, because she would fall asleep in the morning, her husband would be calling her to bed in the evening, and days were too busy. But she knew she needed to do this, so she made coffee and decided to write a record of her thoughts while she read to keep from falling asleep.

Her Bible study books from past ladies' groups had Bible reading guides in the back, so she started to journal the Scripture she read each day along with her thoughts and prayers.

It didn't take long for God to tap her on the shoulder. He said, "Hey, it's rude when having a conversation and you listen to the other person, but then you change the subject altogether!" She had been reading and recording what God said to her, but then she would write about something completely off the subject God was talking about, writing what was on her mind; which was all right, because she was sharing her heart; but God was taking her another step.

So, she began to really look at what God was saying and applying His ideas to her thinking and decisions. Like she had always wondered what Jesus meant when He talked about His body and blood. So when she read in John chapter 6, "Jesus said 'My flesh is real food and My blood is real drink. Whoever eats My flesh and drinks My blood remains in me, and I live in him. Just as the living Father sent Me and I live because of the Father, so the one who feeds on Me will live because of Me'" (verses 55-57).

She had been taught that this was Holy Communion, but she didn't think that was what He meant. Then she read a few verses later where He explains, "The Spirit gives life; the flesh counts for nothing. The words I have spoken to you are spirit and they are life" (verse 63). So real life is spiritual, not physical. Feeding on Christ's body and blood is not eating a piece of bread and taking a drink of wine, the physical, but partaking of His words, which are spiritual, that will nourish the real life we have in Christ; which will also spill over into the physical. Good physical health is a result of good spiritual, mental and emotional health, nourished by God's Word.

So she concluded that her need to get into God's word every day was even more necessary than she had thought!

And she began to see how His Word was practical in everyday living. When she read in Zechariah 7: 9-10, to "show mercy and compassion to one another … in your hearts do not think evil of each other," she was finding that her attitudes toward other people were changing. She developed a desire to see others in a more positive light, to not have uncharitable opinions of other people, even when they are being mean or spiteful. She wanted compassion for them, and to want them to have hope and healing.

And she prayed for the Father to give her His ears to hear what He is saying to her, to understand His ways that are so different from what had been her own ways. And she asked Him to let her see the bigger picture beyond the confines of her own little world.

Then she started to see things in Scripture she never thought was there, to connect the dots and see the connections between things she never thought had anything to do with each other before, like the feasts in the Old Testament and Jesus. There are six feasts God told Israel to celebrate in Exodus, Leviticus, and Deuteronomy, and she was seeing how they laid out Jesus' whole Earthly career.

She could see how Jesus is our (1) Passover, as He is the Passover Lamb slain for us, as I Corinthians 5:7 tells us

And Jesus is the (2) First Fruits of Resurrection, according to I Corinthians 15: 20.

And (3) Pentecost is the birthday of the Church, Jesus's body in Acts 2: 1.

And the (4) Feast of Trumpets would be the Rapture of the Church, at the "last trumpet" in I Corinthians 15: 52, when Jesus calls out His Church.

And nine days after Trumpets is the (5) Day of Atonement. This could be when Jesus returns and cleans up the whole mess of the Earth to set up His Kingdom here.

The last feast is (6) Tabernacles, just five days after the Atonement. This could be our time of rejoicing, celebrating our Divine King and His rule on this Earth while we live in temporary shelters as we build our homes and rebuild the cities in the lands that are now scoured and cleansed.

And all the answers she was finding to her questions about what God's Word was all about was starting to make studying the Bible really exciting!

She had gone through the money she received for selling the Corporation, so she got a job working at an adult sheltered workshop, where she supervised a room of precious mentally and physically disabled young adults. This was very rewarding emotionally, if not very much financially. But it paid the bills.

PART III

CHAPTER 13

A New Start

About that time, Wanda, one of the former student wives from the Bible college, showed up at Babs's church inviting people to go on a medical missionary trip to Rwanda, Africa with A Mother's Hope. This is where the genocide had taken place in 1994 while the world ignored it, and the Hutus murdered as many Tutsis as they could and even many Hutus! Every educated Rwandan was hunted down, and only the very poorest of the people survived.

Since Babs wanted to do missionary work, she signed up, and went to the pre-trip planning meetings. Caryn and Mary were nurses, and Alice was a missionary organizer person, and Wanda's and Caryn's husbands would help in building projects. Babs found out about a medical center in Kansas City that had a lot of "expired" plastic items like cups and spoons (plastic doesn't expire!) she could have to send in the container they were shipping to get there prior to their arrival.

When the time came, they took an all-night flight from Chicago to London, then to Rome. Overnight at a hotel and another early flight to Kigali, the capital of Rwanda. And the airline lost all of their checked luggage! This was Tuesday, and the next flight in wouldn't be in until Saturday night.

Dr. Sam and his brother Peter were from neighboring Nigeria, and they met with them, and provided some insect repellent, toothpaste, and bottled water. The next morning, they came by again to drive them to Cyangugu where his clinic was, up and down mountains through Nyungwe Forest where they saw little black monkeys with white cheeks. When they got to town, they changed some of their money into Rwandan Marks and went shopping for clothes.

At the guest house, the three single ladies had a two-bedroom bungalow with a full bathroom and living room. Mary dropped an earring in the bathroom, and it bounced away, and she couldn't find it. So, the three of them searched every corner of that room and didn't see it at all! Finally, Babs said, "Let's pray about it." They stood arms around each other and prayed: "Father God, we know that You know where that earring is. It's not an important thing, but You are the God of small things, and we are asking You to please help us find her earring." Then they opened their eyes, and there was the earring at their feet in the center of their little circle! He must have had His angel move it there for them to find it!

The next day Dr. Sam had planned out a full itinerary for the nurses, and the rest of the ladies tackled the boxes from the container that had arrived just two days before. Babs found herself sorting out mountains of scrubs and lab coats, folding them onto shelves by size and style.

Babs had met David when they got to the guest house compound and made friends immediately. That night she sat next to him at dinner. He was the bishop from the U. K. who headed up the Anglican Church Welfare Program that was working with A Mother's Hope in Rwanda. They had an enjoyable conversation, and when they were talking about God he seemed to not even be saved, and she was able to share with him some of what God is like and what He's done for us.

The next day they drove out into the rural areas to visit with some of the families in the program, including a lady with elephantiasis with legs swollen so much they completely covered her feet. She lived in a house made of hardened mud, with a thatched roof. The people there were so grateful for even the smallest things that A Mother's Hope provided for them, and Babs realized how spoiled she was as an American.

For lunch they gathered at the church compound where they were served a spread of 8 different items she couldn't even name, all delicious! The afternoon was spent unpacking more boxes while Mary and Caryn taught Dr. Sam and his nurses Basic Precautions and how to use the new items they had for them.

The next day they went to a small village clinic where Caryn treated 65 patients and Babs was invited to sit in on the "counselling" where people talked about the horrors they had endured. It was very therapeutic for the victims to talk about the things that had happened to them, and how they had gotten the victory through Christ. She compassionately listened to ten different people telling their stories; like the girl who had seen her whole family murdered and she was taken as a sex slave, and she forgave her neighbor who did this; and the guy whose home and fields were burned to the ground, and his neighbor who did this now worked with him to plant other fields and build another home. She later compiled them into a notebook she shared with her church back home. She was deeply impressed with God's mercy and grace to these precious people who were able to forgive their perpetrators and still live together in the same neighborhoods, helping one another now as Christians. This was amazing!

Sunday morning came, and they all really enjoyed the service at the Episcopal church that was working with A Mother's Hope in the country. Caryn's husband Gerry preached while Charles interpreted. Then Charles gave an invitation and six men came forward to accept Christ as their Savior! Then those in the church pledged to support these new Christians. It was the most "Baptist" Episcopal service Babs had ever experienced!

After the service, Bishop Geoffrey invited them for muffins and sodas. And they learned that their luggage had arrived. The eight bags that had been lost on Brussels Airlines had come into Kigali on Saturday and were flown to Cyangugu in the morning.

Sunday afternoon they visited the Genocide Memorial at a church where 8,000 were massacred. The girl who kept the key was only eight years old when it happened, and her own parents and family are interred there. It was a very moving experience.

Then their driver Patrick and his wife Scholastical invited them for dinner in their home.

Sunday night the ladies took turns choosing out of some beautiful jewelry that mysteriously showed up in their bags, while some of their personal things had disappeared. It looked like the airport employees had emptied out several groups' bags and put them back together helter-skelter. Caryn's husband Gerry retrieved only one of his pair of sandals.

On Monday they drove to the lake where they canoed to the island. The clinic there didn't even have a doctor, just one nurse and her helpers, and they served thousands without any flowing water or electricity. UNICEF provided some vitamins, but they had no other help besides A Mother's Hope.

That afternoon they emptied some more boxes from the container they had sent, then went back to town to pick up the dress Babs had ordered on Friday, which she wore with the "diamond" necklace from the luggage, to the Grand Supper the Bishop held for them on their last night, which prompted their hosts to call this fair blonde an "African Princess."

The next day they drove back to Kigali where they got the overnight flight to Brussels, Belgium, and from there to Rome. They had opted to spend some time in "first world" after being in "third world" to unwind before coming home. By the time they checked into the bed-and-breakfast in Rome Babs was dog tired and went to bed at eight pm.

Then on Thursday they bought 3-day passes on the city bus and toured Ancient Rome. They saw all the ruins and buildings, the Parthenon, the Colosseum, and lots of excavations. They had lunch at a little table in what seemed to be an alley, which was actually a narrow street! Babs could imagine chariots driving along them between the ancient buildings that were still being used. All over there were beautiful flowers on all the balconies, four and five stories high. Babs thought, "Oh Steve, how much you would have enjoyed the architecture here, especially the high doors you loved so much!" missing him.

They resumed their bus tour the next day at the Colosseum, where they bought that tour also and bypassed all the lines and gave them a lot of information; and it also included the Palladium, the castle of the king, from which they could overlook the Forum, the ancient shopping center and political meeting place. It was huge, the size of a small city. Then they saw the Arch of Titus on the original paving stones of the ancient street. So much history there.

Then, the Metro workers went on strike (so much for their three-day passes!) so that afternoon they rented a car and Gerry, who had previously declared, "I'll never drive in Rome!" had tremendous fun driving them aggressively around in circles! They kept returning to the same monument, the Tomb of the Unknown Soldier. They never did find the Appian Way, but they all enjoyed the thrilling two-hour "tour" of Rome! They eventually did find their way back to the bed-and-breakfast, from the opposite direction.

On Saturday they booked a tour to Naples and Pompeii, a four-hour bus drive each way, an all-day excursion, and got back after 9:30 pm. Kevin and Wanda got off the bus downtown to have a romantic dinner the last night in Rome, and Babs wistfully thought about Steve, and the missed opportunities that would never happen now.

The three single ladies were the last passengers on the bus. Mary (the "man magnet") talked the driver into taking them closer than the Crown Center Hotel, but he couldn't take his huge bus onto the little street their place was on, so they walked the 2 meters (Alice's estimate) to their bed-and-breakfast.

The next morning was back to the airport in Rome to fly to Heathrow in London and catch the all-night flight to Chicago then into Kansas City.

Babs spent that flying time thinking about how spoiled she was living in the United States. And what could she do for the Rwandans if she ever returned? One of their biggest problems was getting clean water. Maybe she could research that when she got home.

Babs finally got home and was able to climb into bed by 2:00 am, but she was up again at 8:00 am! She showered, drank coffee without any sugar or creamer, unpacked most of her luggage, saw Alice and Mary when they came to pick up their cars they'd left in Babs' parking area, went to Wal-Mart to have her four rolls of film developed, went through the two-weeks mail that had piled up, and several other things that needed to be done.

While Babs was on the other side of the world, Naomi, her first-born, was planning her wedding! Being very independent and self-sufficient, she wanted the whole show to be her own, so the only thing she allowed her mom to do was to provide the venue and make the wedding cake!

So Babs slept nine hours Monday night, after the trip, and was up again on Tuesday at 8:00 am. She met with her Ladies Bible Study that night, and Wednesday was up at 6:00 am to be at Naomi's by 8:00 am to pick up her Wedding Dress, and her own Mother of the Bride Dress. She was bouncing with energy! She'd never had energy like this at home before. Maybe this is what God made her for, to be a foreign missionary!

Babs spent the next two days baking and frosting her daughter's wedding cake, to be decorated with fresh flowers Friday morning before the wedding. Since the back yard was like a park, the chairs were set up in the shelter for the ceremony, and then the guests all gathered in the recreation room of the building for the reception. It was beautiful.

Babs continued to journal her Bible studies and prayers every day, and after a while noticed all her filled journals stacking up. She wondered, "What's going to happen to them when I'm gone? The kids will find them and say, 'Huh, Mom's journals!' and toss them into a box. These contain good Bible studies, things God's been teaching me, that others need to know! What can I do with them?"

About that time, her sister Janet's daughter out in California who was a pastry chef, put on Facebook, "Look, I'm blogging my recipes!" Babs clicked on the link and was taken right to it! "Wow, that's cool! A blog, huh? I don't know anything about blogs, I'll Google it."

Babs found a chart of about a dozen different blog platforms, showing all the different features offered. She tried a couple of them, and found one that she could work with, and started to put her journal entries into blog posts! This was fun!

She typed up three or four that first day, then a couple of days later, two or three more. Then every couple of days or when the thought struck her, she'd put up another, or even two or three or more. She wasn't very consistent with her blog, not like her quiet times every day.

One day she noticed that she hadn't done much with her blog at all for quite a while, and she thought, "If I'm going to do this, I have to be more consistent. I read the Bible every day, what if someone's reading my blog for their quiet time? I'll need to put one up every day. But only one every day."

Babs didn't know how long she could do this, because she was so inconsistent, but if this is what God wanted her to do, then she'd have to do it in His strength and faithfulness.

She started to put one post on her blog every day. Sometimes she could look at her schedule and see that she'd be really busy the next day, and found that she could schedule the publication of her blog at a different day and time; so, she could sometimes do todays entry, then schedule tomorrows to post when she couldn't do it then, and still have one published every day.

God did give her the perseverance and faithfulness to continue to publish a new post every day, for several years! When Babs realized how long she'd done this, she amazed herself with God's faithfulness to her. And her readership extended all over the world!

Babs had met Shodree at a mutual friend's birthday party. She appreciated Babs' joyful playfulness and invited her to her husband's surprise birthday party. Babs was sick with a cold, and Shodree had a broken ankle, but they were the only two dancing to the music at the party! As their friendship progressed, Shodree also recognized Babs' compassionate heart, and hired her to help care for a 98-year-old former missionary lady in her home. Now Babs was a caregiver, too.

After the missionary lady passed away, Shodree sent Babs to care for other elderly people in their homes from time to time, working part-time. This income helped to pay the bills.

Meanwhile, Babs was living in that mansion inside the commercial building alone, with her children having grown up and left to make their own lives. She decided that it would be a good time to sell it and take that world-wide vagabonding trip she had dreamed about to share the Good News of the Gospel with people in other nations. Since her days at the Bible college, she'd been wanting to do missionary work, but Steve was called to business. Now that she was relatively unencumbered, maybe she could use the funds from the property for her travels. So, she put it on the market, as a commercial property. Steve had gotten a variance from the city to be able to move the family in, and Babs was grandfathered in after she sold the business.

Soon a prospective buyer came by with the realtor. They thought it would be perfect to move their business into and contacted the city to weave their way through all the paperwork. But every department head in the maze of government wanted to get his finger into the pie, and the prospective buyer pulled out.

This happened again. And again. Then the contract was up, and Babs tacked up a sign on the front fence, "For Sale By Owner" with a description and phone number. But never got a call.

She got another realtor, and tried it again, but the same thing happened again. Every prospective buyer was being told they needed to do something else, different from every other, always too expensive for these small businesses to be able to do.

So, she just sat for a while, still working for Shodree from time to time, and having her quiet times with God. "Well, Father, I guess it just isn't Your time for me to travel the world. But I will wait on You to show me what you would have me do, in Your time."

Babs was still blogging and had gone through many journals following the Our Daily Bread reading guides from RBC Ministries in Grand Rapids, Michigan that her church made available. She had read through the Bible several times through the years, but when she joined a Bible study group at church studying through the whole Bible together in a year and journaling, that's when she began to realize how it all fits together into one story. Then she also began to blog through whole books of the Bible, or whole ideas traced through the Bible.

When Babs thought about when she first tried to read the Bible, she couldn't understand it at all. Now God's Holy Spirit in her was teaching her so much. She had really come far, one step at a time, over the years.

God was showing her so many connections between the various dots of information in His word. She even made an Excel chart of the whole book of Revelation, just to try to understand some of the confusing events that couldn't possibly happen twice at two different times.

CHAPTER 14

A New Leg in the Journey—
Turning the Corner

Then the city had a change of administration, and the new city fathers started to look at what the laws actually said, instead of just going by whatever FEMA decreed in Washington. And another realtor called her wanting to list the place.

He said, "Miss Watson, because you have been living here continually for so long, as long as you don't move out more than three months before someone else moves in, it can also be advertised as residential. Since this place has more than one street address, we can list it in both the commercial and the residential listings."

This was good news! Before they had told her that no one else could ever live there again because it sat on Town Creek, a 100-year flood plain, as per FEMA guidelines. Now, because Babs was still living there, anyone who wanted to live there could buy it as residential. As long as she didn't leave it vacant for 3 months, for then it would revert back to commercial only again.

Soon a young couple with teenaged children were looking through the compound wide-eyed! The husband said that he had watched as Steve had built the house, and when it was featured in the local paper, he saw the tall doors with obscure glass in the master bathroom, and had been looking for doors like them for years. When they were able to buy the property, he could hardly believe that those very doors were his now!

Babs realized that God had brought the perfect family who would realize what a monstrous job the compound was to take care of and maintain, and to love it and care for it the way it needed, the way Steve had.

And fifteen years after Babs first put it on the market, it finally sold!

Now what will she do? Will she put all her stuff into storage and travel? Will she rent a small place or buy a house? She talked with God again and searched for His answer.

Babs' older daughter and her husband had been busy through these years growing their family. They lived near the church, which was two towns away from where Babs lived.

Naomi was home-schooling all four of her children online, while she herself took college classes from Liberty University, also online. Every year for several years she talked about moving to Virginia to take her Doctorate classes on-campus, after she earned her Bachelor's and Master's, but she and her husband were still working on the house they were in to get it up to selling standards.

So, Babs didn't know how long she would be able to see her grandkids.

Babs wanted to be near her family while she could before they left town. As the kids' only Grandma she wanted to be able to have the opportunity to pour into their lives if she could.

So, Babs decided to buy a house of her own, and found a beautiful little 3-bedroom on a quiet street near her daughter and her church, and moved her furniture in. She had rented a U-Haul trailer and some wardrobe boxes, and her grandchildren came over to help her pack everything into boxes obtained from Menards and some of the men at her church helped with the heavy things.

With the proceeds from the sale of her commercial compound she was able to pay cash for the house, so there wouldn't be any mortgage, and she also paid off her car. So, she was debt-free!

She started to make this new house into her home, making the second bedroom a guest room with the old fold-out bed-couch she had since her kids were little, and she bought an entertainment center from the Thrift store for the T.V. to which she hooked up the VHS and Disk player for her grandchildren to enjoy when they stayed overnight. She made the third bedroom into her office, with a beautiful roll-top desk, also from the Thrift store, as well as several nice book cases.

"Well, hello! Who are you, pretty kitty? Do you belong to somebody? You're just hanging around on my back deck, meowing like you're hungry." The previous owners must have abandoned him, poor dear.

He was a beautiful black, long-haired cat with yellow eyes, and the sweetest face. Babs didn't even have the water turned on yet, that first day, but the cat seemed skittish, and wouldn't let her near it. The next day he was still on the deck off the kitchen, and she put bowls of cat food and water out for him. She also bought a little wrought-iron table and chairs and sat there quietly so he could approach safely. It didn't take long for him to sit on her lap and let her pet him.

Since he was all black, she decided to call him Ebony, and he even came inside during the days. But when the sun was nearing the horizon, he wanted to go outside again.

That first summer Babs was able to hire a neighbor to keep her yard mowed and weed-eated. She didn't have Steve anymore, and couldn't depend on anyone else to take care of its maintenance, so she had to get to know this house she'd bought. She had to adopt Steve's mantra: "If it is to be, it's up to me!" She always had lived by, "If I don't do it, maybe somebody else will!" But there was no one else. This was not Steve's house, it was Babs' own house, and she was the only one who would be caring for it. Since she was a child of the King, as His princess this would be her temporary palace, and her only servant to help her make it so was herself! This was a complete turn-around for Babs.

"Well, I guess I really will have to grow up, now!" She still wanted to vagabond the world, spreading the seed of the Gospel, but she lived a lot closer to her grandchildren now, and they grow up so fast.

Babs had been spending two or three nights a week with an elderly lady, a client, who was 92 years old whose children knew she wanted to stay in her own home. Her daughter-in-law had inherited her mother's house and gave all the lace curtains from it to Babs, to put up all over her new house to beautify the windows. It already had carpeting in the bedrooms, and Babs put her Persian rugs out on them and in the living room. And she hung some of her many pictures on the bare walls. It was shaping up to be a nice home.

When Christmas was approaching, the grandkids offered to put up her Christmas Tree for her, so she had to get one! Naomi had bought a bigger one for their living room, and gave the "old" one to Babs, so the kids already knew how to put it all together. Then they stayed over Christmas Eve and opened presents in the morning. Their mom had already "hidden" their presents at Grandma's house!

Babs wanted to spend more time with her grandkids, so she got them a new board game for

Christmas and made them leave it there at Grand-ma's, to come over every week for Game Day and play it there. So, it became a weekly date and some-times they would stay overnight then, too.

Now and then when her daughter and son-in-law wanted a week-end away Babs would take the kids, letting the two older girls sleep on the fold-out couch she got for the living room while the two younger ones slept in the guest room. The hall bathroom was theirs, with the full tub, and Babs showered in her master bath.

One spring morning early at first light there was knocking on Babs' door. "I'm your neighbor, do you have your cat?" Babs went to the deck door where Ebony waited to come in each morning and called him. There was no sign of him.

"Well, there's a cat on the road out front; it's dead. It looks like yours."

"Uhhh!" Babs ran out barefoot in her nightgown, and sure enough, it was Ebony, flat as a pancake! Oh poor kitty! He was a black cat on a black street on a black night, and the pick-up driver just didn't see him. She went back in and got dressed. When she called Animal Control they told her, "We don't take care of dead animals, just live ones."

"Then what should I do with him?"

"Pick it up and throw it away!"

Babs couldn't just "throw him away," he needed to be buried. So she got an old sheet, wrapped him in it, and picked him up with her snow shovel. Then she called her daughter in tears: "I don't even have a shovel to bury him!"

So, Naomi and the grandkids came over with shovels and they all worked together to put him in a grave in the back corner of the back yard. Then they all stood around the grave and honored him with a little "funeral service," each saying something about him. The kids even made him a gravestone!

"Grandma, we can get you another kitty! Do you want several? Our friend's cat had a litter out on their farm, we can get you 6 or 8!"

"No, no, I don't want another cat the same day I bury him."

She had Prince Ebony for a year, from one spring to the next. She needed to wait a while before she could replace him.

That second summer, Babs hired her lawncare out again, but the expense of it was getting harder to justify. The 92-year-old lady had died peacefully in her own bed, which deprived Babs of that income, and Social Security never even came close to being enough. And her savings account was also dwindling, even with just the utilities and other ongoing expenses. She started to think about what she could do to support herself while travelling. She could write a book. But how long would that take, and how long before it would pay her anything?

The grandkids still wanted to get her replacements for her pet, but she told them she'd only want one or two cats, no more. Since they wanted to surprise her, they showed up the day after Thanksgiving with a pet carrier—with two beautiful grey-striped kittens that were sisters from the same litter. "Merry Christmas, Grandma! What are you going to name them?"

"Well, this one has tiger stripes, so I'll call her Tigress; and the other one has a really fluffy coat so I'll call her Fluffy." And Babs again had feline company. She decided that these kitties would stay inside, so she set up the finished basement room as theirs, put a sand-box in the half-bath down there, and put a hook on the door so they couldn't paw it open during the night.

And the grandkids got them Christmas presents, too.

Meanwhile, she met a new friend at church who needed a place to stay and she offered her guest room. So, Marika came to stay temporarily and she enjoyed her friendship with Babs so much she decided to rent the room monthly!

The grandkids were still coming over every Thursday afternoon for Game Day at Grandmas, and when Marika bought a T.V. and put it in the living room, the kids enjoyed watching programs on Grandma's Amazon Prime when they spent nights there.

She had continued to study the Bible and add another post to her blog every day, and she had also put her series of studies through one of the epistles into book form and self-published it online.

Then she started on her second book. When her books began to sell, she'd be able to do that vagabonding the world to spread the seed of the Gospel when her family moves away.

And Marika offered to manage the house and rent out the guestroom as an Airbnb for a little additional income for Babs while she travelled.

So, God made everything fall into place perfectly for Babs, as she waited on Him and trusted His care for her. She continued her daily blog and to write Bible-study books; and when Naomi moved away, Babs' books were selling, so she was finally able to take off and go to serve God as a missionary, and work to promote the Kingdom of God, travelling and writing and speaking all over the world.

She saw lives changing, and broken people healed, and God's family increasing as sinners repented and turned to the Lord for Salvation. Until He comes.

Even so, come Lord Jesus!

Thank You for Reading My Book!

I really appreciate all your feedback,
and I love hearing what you have to say.

I need your input to make the next version
of this book and my future books better.

Please leave me an honest review on Amazon
letting me know what you thought of the book.

Thanks so much!

Bonnie Werner

Self-Publishing
School

NOW IT'S YOUR TURN
Discover the EXACT 3-step
blueprint you need to become
a bestselling author in as little as 3 months.

Self-Publishing School helped me,
and now I want them to help you with this FREE
resource to begin outlining your book!

Even if you're busy, bad at writing,
or don't know where to start,
you CAN write a bestseller
and build your best life.

With tools and experience across a variety of
niches and professions,
Self-Publishing School
is the only resource you need
to take your book to the finish line!

DON'T WAIT

Say "YES" to becoming a bestseller:

https://self-publishingschool.com/friend/

Follow the steps on the page to get a FREE
resource to get started on your book
and unlock a discount to get started with Self-Publishing School